A Nest of Magic

Kate Moseman

Fortunella Press

ISBN 978-1-957320-29-8

In all things of nature there is something of the marvelous.

—Aristotle

I

There once was a town where nothing ever happened—until, one day, it did.

It all began the day that Corinthia, the librarian of Shadow Ridge, maneuvered the rolling cart of free books outside the library's front doors, positioning it for a good view from patrons who would walk by or perhaps pull up in the drop off lane. A whole education could be had from the free books, she thought. A chaotic education, to be sure, consisting of everything from nineteenth-century literature to introductory woodworking, but an education all the same.

Though the late October weather could be unpredictable, on this day the air was crisp, the sky was clear and blue, and Corinthia would have rather been inside anyway.

She dusted off her hands and went inside, choosing one of the two solid, normal doors that flanked the central revolving door. Secretly, Corinthia found the revolving door slightly alarming, and felt safer using the plain doors, though she would have not admitted it to anyone—except, perhaps, her best friend, Stevie.

Stevie worked at the Shadow Ridge Environmental Center, which shared a building with the Shadow Ridge Library. The Shadow Ridge Environmental Center oversaw a tiny, two-room museum and a four-hundred acre nature preserve of Florida scrubland known as the Refuge.

At the moment, Stevie wasn't in the museum, or the Refuge; she was in one of the swivel chairs behind the library's circulation desk, where she wasn't supposed to be, and she was industriously spinning herself in circles.

Stevie's sheer energy made her seem to take up more space than her actual size. She wore crisp t-shirts with environmentally-themed art, and her hair was perpetually pulled into a high ponytail that bounced with every movement.

Corinthia wore her hair pulled back as well, but low and contained. Her t-shirts were billboards for library services. There was not a language learning program, a free movie-streaming platform, or a subscription to seven thousand newspapers and periodicals for which Corinthia did not have a shirt. When paired with dark wash jeans and low-key but impeccably clean sneakers, it made a most efficient approach to workwear.

"Aren't you supposed to be feeding the snakes or something?" Corinthia asked, sliding into the adjacent chair and putting one foot on Stevie's seat to stop the dizzying rotation.

"I fed the snakes, and the turtles, and the baby alligators. And I dusted the taxidermied hawk, and I tidied the brochures and the trail maps, and now I'm here because here is more fun."

Corinthia pushed Stevie's chair, spinning it slowly, like a heavy globe. "And how is here more fun, exactly?"

"There are people here."

Corinthia surveyed the view. The circulation desk was currently decorated with paper pumpkins and sprays of artificial autumn leaves. From the behind the desk, she could see from the front doors to the stacks of fiction and nonfiction; across the room to the reference desk, above which dozens of colorful origami birds dangled from strings attached to the ceiling; all the way to the life-sized artificial tree hung with warm white lights in the children's section. Donated claw-foot bathtubs sat on the floor beneath its branches like boats left on the sand at low tide, each one filled with pillows to create a cozy reading nook perfectly sized for a child. Corinthia knew they were perfectly sized for a child because she had climbed into one to try it out, and, disappointingly, her long, sturdy legs had had to hang over the sides.

Oh, yes, and there were people. People moving through the stacks, tapping on computer keyboards, turning pages, opening and closing the copier lid, all the usual activity of the just-opened library like warm blood in Corinthia's veins, healthy and purposeful.

The Shadow Ridge Library had comfortable chairs, sensibly carpeted floors, thoughtfully-sized tables for working in groups, and even a collection of little rooms off to the sides available to borrow for quiet and privacy by the hour. This was how a library should be designed: from the inside, with patrons' needs considered first.

Not too far away, an old library had been torn down and replaced with an architectural marvel that, despite its exterior beauty, had clearly not been designed for the use of actual people. Slippery polished concrete everywhere; awkward chairs; terrible flights of stairs that left access for people with disabilities a complete afterthought. Corinthia heartily disapproved. What good was beauty if it actively harmed those it was supposed to serve?

Her library dispensed with such pretensions. There were large plastic letters on the wall that spelled out "Check It Out!" above the circulation desk, and another set that spelled out "Look It Up!" above the self-service library catalog computers. A glowing neon sign indicated "The Teen Zone" in a style that was neither new nor fashionable, but it was most certainly eye-catching.

Stevie had stopped spinning and was staring at a woman in the new book section. The woman wore a fitted black tank top and loose cargo pants. Her biceps flexed as she picked up one book or another. Every movement of her sculpted arm muscles rippled colorful and extensive tattoos, which were made even more arresting by what appeared to be a light sheen of body oil that brought out the nuances of the ink. Stevie seemed to be riveted.

"I told you—just *talk* to her," Corinthia said, observing her friend's pining. "She won't bite."

Stevie shook her head vehemently. "She's too cool. Look at her, with her muscles and her tattoos and her…. well, every-thing," Stevie finished, with a sigh.

"I'll introduce you." Corinthia knew the woman's name was Drew, that she was a transplanted New Yorker, that she ran a food truck that frequently visited the Shadow Ridge Library, and that she was a handywoman and a marriage officiant on the side, to make a little extra cash.

"What do you think she'll check out?" Stevie asked.

Corinthia, as a rule, did not approve of discussing patron book selections, but could make an exception if she knew the person in question would gladly have shared the information themselves. Corinthia and Drew had cordially traded book recommendations, on occasion, and thus Corinthia knew that Drew favored sci-fi romances. Corinthia shared this fact with Stevie.

"I wonder if they're the kind where you turn the pages and smoke comes out," Stevie mused, with another besotted sigh.

Corinthia smiled to herself. "I'll make you a deal."

"What's that?"

"If you pluck up your courage and speak to her when she comes to check out, I'll go for a walk in the Refuge."

Stevie sat up straight and stared at Corinthia in open shock. "But—you hate the outdoors! You've lived here more than a decade and you've never even set foot in the Refuge!"

In fact, Corinthia's house was situated on the far side of the Refuge, directly up against the nature preserve and separated from it only by her own wooden fence. But Corinthia only looked out on the Refuge, whether from her back window or from the library's conservatory windows, and never entered it. The Refuge was faintly menacing foliage; the indoors was air-conditioned safety, and that was where Corinthia liked to stay. Wilderness had beauty but also unpredictability; unpredictability was best kept securely inside the cover of a good book, where it could not leach into real life and cause pandemonium.

"Correction," Corinthia said. "I don't hate the outdoors. I hate *being* in the outdoors. I hate bugs. I despise snakes. I loathe creepy-crawlies in general."

"But you'll really do it? You'll go for a hike in the Refuge?"

"Let's not call it a hike. I'm allergic to hikes. Let's call it a short, gentle stroll."

"Corinthia, if you go a round dozen *steps* into the Refuge, I will buy you lunch."

"Then it's a deal." She put out her hand and her best friend shook it.

Then they waited while Drew continued to browse.

The origami birds trembled. The lights in the artificial tree branches twinkled. Children climbed into the bathtubs and disappeared, only their hands and books visible floating over the rims of the tubs. Corinthia busied herself with the myriad tasks of the circulation desk.

So many people thought librarians were just keepers of books, but they were so much more. To be a librarian was to find out what people needed, and connect them to it. In the old days it might have been a canister of microfiche or the right volume in the law library. Nowadays it might be video game clubs to encourage teen literacy; having a social worker stationed in the library to help the down-and-out; or co-hosting a Wildlife Festival with the Shadow Ridge Environmental Center.

And then the revolving door twirled, and a wind of change entered the library—along with a person.

"*Who* is *that*?" Stevie said, quietly.

Corinthia, who had been focused on the computer screen and some minor technical malfunction, looked up.

Out of the library entryway she swooped: a petite woman in a billowing blue dress that looked and fluttered like silk; her hair silver-gray and topped with an elaborate jeweled comb. Her face was lively, neither young nor old, perhaps—like Corinthia—in her mid- to late thirties. Though at a distance her eyes were dark, even still they were lit, like the night sky, with the sparkle of stars. She swept past the circulation desk and the soft breeze of her passing caressed Corinthia's cheek.

Part of Corinthia wanted to stop time—stop the revolving door, stop the revolving Earth, even—just to look at her a little longer. But another part of her knew it would be like trying to hold a wild bird in the palm of her hand. Unreasonable, unthinkable. A wish and a dream, sweet and fleeting, no more.

Corinthia realized her mouth was open when her lips went dry.

Who was that?

Stevie was frantically nudging Corinthia under the table, which reminded Corinthia to close her mouth and try to act normal as she scanned another patron's selections and printed a receipt.

When they were alone again, Stevie piped up. "Did you see her?" She peered at Corinthia's face. "Am I crazy, or were you kind of checking her out?"

Corinthia was far above checking out patrons, unless it was in a literal sense, with books. Even patrons in fairy-tale gemstones and soft-looking silk. Corinthia pointedly ignored Stevie.

"You were!" Stevie said, delightedly. "You know," she added, as if reflecting on something especially satisfying, "I enjoy these occasional reminders that the great and wise Corinthia has tender emotions just like the rest of us."

Corinthia ignored this as well and instead pointed out that Drew was approaching with a handful of books.

Stevie patted her hair and pinched her cheeks quickly, then crossed her legs, uncrossed them, and finally settled on tucking one leg under and swinging the other in what she probably hoped was an unbothered, carefree manner.

"Good morning, Drew," Corinthia said.

Drew smiled. "Hey," she said, a sharp lift of her chin including Stevie in the greeting. Her gruff way of speaking could at first frighten the timid, but Drew's few words were because she was a rare good listener, who opened her ears before she opened her mouth.

Stevie's eyelashes fluttered.

"Did you find everything you were looking for?" Corinthia said, politely but with an extra helping of warmth, out of loyalty to Stevie and a desire to prolong the conversation as a good wingwoman should.

Drew leaned on the circulation desk and pushed a short stack of books across the surface. "These," she said. "But I was looking for the sequel to this." She handed Corinthia a single title: *Alien Space Lesbians*. An intensely purple, humanoid woman with scaly skin graced the cover.

Stevie's eyebrows shot up.

Corinthia took the cue. "Drew, this is my friend, Stevie. Stevie works next door at the environmental center. Stevie, this is Drew. She runs the Drew's D-Lites food truck."

"Pleased to meet you, Drew," Stevie said, adding more eyelash flutters in case the first spasm hadn't been clear enough.

"Likewise," Drew said, adding a slow, warm smile.

Corinthia had to interrupt the mutual admiration session by clearing her throat. "Looks like it's still on order. Would you like me to put a hold on it for you, so you'll be first in line to get it when it arrives?"

"Please."

"Can you put a hold on it for me, too?" Stevie asked. "After Drew, of course."

"Of course," Corinthia said, wondering how people managed to flirt so easily. She'd dated a bit, but almost always on a setup from a mutual friend, and even then the matches never managed to ignite. "Did you want this one?" She held up *Alien Space Lesbians.*

"Nah," Drew said. "I memorized it."

"I'll put it back for you then." Corinthia finished checking out Drew's books and stood up. Suddenly, a great crash arose from the stacks. "Excuse me," Corinthia said, and hurried out from behind the desk in the direction of the noise, carrying

Alien Space Lesbians as she passed through the low bookcases of the reference section.

Local sculptures marched across the top of the bookcases. Corinthia particularly liked the pelican, the sea turtle, and something that resembled a multi-headed sea worm. Corinthia had spent a lot of time thinking about what that one might mean; looking up its actual meaning would have possibly been a disappointment, so she chose to remain in contemplative ignorance.

She rounded a corner of the shelves and found the woman in blue surrounded by a flock of fallen books.

"I'm *so* sorry," the woman said. "I was trying to carry too many, and..." Her hands fluttered.

"Not a problem," Corinthia said, immediately stooping to gather books. She had to set *Alien Space Lesbians* on a shelf first to free both hands.

When they had both straightened up, the woman in blue picked up the sci-fi romance and admired the cover. "How lovely!" she said. She looked at Corinthia. "You're a *librarian*, aren't you?"

She said it with the kind of solemn admiration people usually saved for doctors, the Peace Corps, or the clergy, and Corinthia's cheeks warmed from the unexpected admiration.

"Yes," she said, unable to come up with anything more clever to say, or to flutter her eyelashes as Stevie had.

The stars in the woman's eyes sparkled. "And did *you* acquire this particular book for the library?"

"Yes," Corinthia lied, helplessly. The county office made most of the purchasing decisions, but under the woman's gaze Corinthia could not help but grasp at the halo of her approval, while secretly entertaining a shy hope that her own approval of sapphic romance would speak for itself.

"How lovely," the woman repeated, as with one elegant finger she traced the contours of the cover art, and Corinthia somehow felt the touch run down her spine. "What's it about?"

Corinthia looked down at the cover, hoping for a hint to help her brazen it out. There was the purple alien with scaly skin—and, Corinthia now noticed, a tiny set of delicate horns—and she held in her embrace an attractive but clearly human woman. There were stars all around, and they both seemed extremely happy.

"It's a story," Corinthia said, "of two women from very different worlds, who fall in love despite the odds." She met the woman's gaze, which was unfortunately like falling into a plunge pool where her feet couldn't touch the bottom. She thrashed her way back to self-mastery and librarianship. "Did you want to check it out?"

The woman leaned in slightly, and whispered as if sharing a delightful secret: "I can't." She followed this up with a wink, which left Corinthia completely at sea. "I'll just read it here."

Stevie bounded up behind Corinthia. "I just came to see if you needed any help," she said. "By the way, I'm Stevie! And this is Corinthia. It's nice to meet you..." She looked at the woman in blue expectantly, and Corinthia had the vague impression that Stevie had not in fact come to help pick up the books but to help with something else entirely.

"I'm Rosemary," the woman said.

"What an unusual name," Stevie said, clearly satisfied by her own introduction ploy. "Isn't that an unusual name, Corinthia?"

"No more so than 'Corinthia,'" she replied, hoping Rosemary would not be offended.

"Then we have something in common," Rosemary replied. "Nice to meet you, Stevie." She paused, reserving a smile full of secrets for the librarian of Shadow Ridge. "And you, Corinthia."

2

After Rosemary disappeared, Corinthia and Stevie returned to the circulation desk. Stevie took a seat and bounced up and down in her chair like an overenthusiastic kangaroo. "Did you *see* her? Did you see how she looked at you?"

Corinthia's composure wrapped her like a weighted blanket. "I don't flirt with patrons," she said. "It's not professional. Besides, don't you have a snake to keep company?"

"Come on, Corinthia. She likes romance novels. You like romance novels. This isn't difficult."

"Romance novels aren't real."

"They sure are. I've seen the bookshelves at your house."

"Yes," Corinthia replied, severely. "Because books don't disappoint. People do."

Stevie crossed her arms and stared at Corinthia. "You're a curmudgeon."

"Yes," Corinthia said, and then busied herself organizing the interior of a desk drawer.

Stevie spun around in the office chair. "You're a curmudgeon who has to walk through the Refuge, though."

"Go tend to your snakes and taxidermied hawks."

"Hawk, singular. There's only one." Stevie hopped up, leaving the chair still spinning. But before she left, she threw an unexpected arm around Corinthia's shoulders. "Lunch is on me tomorrow."

"From Drew's food truck," Corinthia said.

"Where else? And then you can tell me all about your hike." Stevie left, back to the Shadow Ridge Environmental Center and its resident reptiles.

There were many things to do that day, and Corinthia did them all. Among her duties, she had made a pastime of managing the printer. She had carefully printed out and pasted on the machine a sign that said, "Do not use your own paper or attempt to clear a paper jam! Please see someone at the Reference Desk." Which was misleading, because they would pick up the phone and dial Corinthia's extension, and Corinthia would stand over the machine with all the authority of Moses parting the Red Sea, and the machine would tremble before

her and immediately disgorge its hastily and ill-advisedly gob-
bled paper. Everyone knew she had a knack.

While busy with tasks, she did not let herself consider that
she was also looking for Rosemary, who had disappeared along
with the romance novel despite never seeming to pass by the
circulation desk.

At the end of the day Corinthia approached the settling of
the bet like she would any other slightly unappealing business:
calmly, professionally, the only sign of reluctance an unusual
urge to clear her throat repeatedly.

She pushed open a back door—staff use only—and found
herself on the sidewalk that outlined the back of the Shadow
Ridge Library. This concrete ribbon faced the forbidding wall
of skinny live oaks that surrounded the Refuge.

A local artist had painted the exterior of the library to match
the Refuge itself: twisted oak trees climbed the walls in a
perfect mirror of the landscape. If Corinthia squinted, the
Shadow Ridge Library and the Refuge merged. Only with
eyes wide open could they be separated, the Refuge with its
more muted colors, the library walls vivid in their mimicry.
What if, Corinthia thought, the Refuge decided to camouflage
itself with books tucked into the trees in neat rows? Instead of

the Dewey Decimal System, everything would be arranged by Forest Figural Filing.

"I changed my mind," Corinthia said, to no one in particular.

The door clanged shut behind her, locked.

If she wanted to go back inside the library, she would have to follow the sidewalk all the way around to the front of the building, past the miniature museum and Stevie. And then she would have to tell Stevie the truth—that she'd been too chicken to go in. Lying wasn't Corinthia's way, mostly because she wasn't good at it, and it gave her a stomach pain.

"Fine," Corinthia said, speaking to Stevie, the sky, and whatever snakes might be frightened away by the sound of her voice. "I'm going."

Corinthia followed the outdoor path through the Pollinator Garden. She loved its orderly stone paths and carefully tended beds of native plants. There was a bench beneath an arbor, and a wall-mounted pair of painted scrub jay wings for taking souvenir pictures. All in all a most restful place, and with no more dangers or unpredictability than a drowsy bumblebee getting lost on its way to the beautyberry bushes.

The Pollinator Garden overlooked the Outdoor Amphitheater, which was of such a generous size—it could hold seven hundred people—that it often took visitors by surprise when they first saw it. The amphitheater was something Corinthia took a secret pride in, though she of course had not built it, because it was so clearly intended for the community as an object of pure enjoyment and enrichment. Concerts and theatrical productions sent a thrum of excitement through the very foundation of the entire complex, and probably into the Refuge as well. Corinthia wondered if the birds minded.

Down the path from the Outdoor Amphitheater, there was a large sign marked with trails. The main trails looped through the Refuge in a series of ever-greater tracks, the smallest nested inside the next largest, nested inside the longest trail that went all the way to the back, along the border of Corinthia's neighborhood. Corinthia took a photo of the map, then stepped down from the sidewalk, her shoes landing softly on the dirt.

A footpath of dirt mixed with dead leaves led from the sidewalk to the trees, but it disappeared around a corner immediately, providing no view of the inside of the nature preserve.

"Better not be any snakes," she muttered, and then turned the corner.

The air pressed in, held close by the trees. The canopy muted the sunlight, and the scent of dead leaves rose as they were crushed underfoot. The path dipped and rose like a children's roller coaster.

Corinthia thought of an airlock.

The dirt path transitioned from gray to an almost unnatural white, the same color as the sand on the shores of Sparkle Beach, over thirty miles to the east. Gaps appeared in the tree canopy, providing a peek at the sky above the trail. The taller trees gave way to short ones—these were more like tangled, overgrown shrubs than trees, but they were still tall enough not to be able to see over them.

Corinthia felt she had left the airlock and had entered something entirely different. Between the white sand and the green walls of low trees on either side of the path, the path before her looked like the first arm of a maze.

"Castle Adventure," she mused, a childhood memory coming back in flashes. A building like a medieval castle, complete with turrets and a decorative portcullis. Children rushing through the lobby on the way to the birthday rooms, for obligatory pizza before the real attraction of Castle Adventure: a life-size labyrinth made of wooden panels. The panels were so tall even parents couldn't see over them, and the walls were moved around every so often, so that even if you had found your way before, the way would be different the next time.

Once inside, you either found your way to the center, or you gave up and followed the yellow-painted arrows on the ground, which led you through a series of designated emergency-exit panels all the way back to the entrance. No one spent much time on pizza at Castle Adventure. Everyone wanted to be the first to reach the center of the maze.

But there were no yellow-painted arrows here. No movable panels. Only a blindingly white sand path hemmed by walls of greenery.

Corinthia could not shake the strange feeling that she'd left an airlock only to find herself at the bottom of the sea. The white sand beneath her feet and the blue sky above conspired to create a feeling of great depth, and Corinthia was reminded that much of the state had once been underwater.

The library was gone. It may as well never have existed. To look around was to have no evidence at all that *anything* existed except for this.

Somewhere in the distance, a vigilant cry of "Kweep!" jumped from point to point, as if it wasn't different birds but one bird with the ability to teleport.

Corinthia had never heard this cry before.

She came upon a rack of walking staves in time to steady herself against the undersea sensation playing havoc with her sense of balance. She picked one up, gave it an experimental swing, then planted the narrower end in the sand and walked on.

This wasn't so bad, she thought. She'd be done with the loop and back in the library in no time. And there would be a delicious lunch with Stevie on Friday.

But other, wordless thoughts settled to the bottom of her mind, restless and contradictory: a feeling of being both ill at ease and home at last.

Corinthia walked on, the staff thudding crisply into the sand.

Smaller white sand paths squiggled off into the underbrush. All the trails added up to turns in the maze, unidentifiable, nothing like the clearly marked trails on the map. While Corinthia tried to make sense of it, a bird called out from the left.

"Kweep!" it said, cheery and alert.

"Kweep!" said another, this time from straight ahead.

She couldn't help but imagine that this was funny to them, to watch her blunder her way through their territory. Which way was the library? Which way was her house? On what side was the road that led from the library to her neighborhood?

Corinthia huffed up a small incline, disoriented.

At the top of the hill the elevation was enough to reveal great sweeps of the maze below her. Corinthia tried to take pictures, one after another, but as soon as the landscape was caught on her phone, it flattened into a dull, unremarkable scene. The sand no longer looked so white. The path didn't swoop up and down. The trees, so strange in their tangled walls, could have been a heap of overgrown weeds. If you saw those pictures, you would have argued against the idea that there was anything even slightly special about it. It was as if the Refuge had its own camouflage.

Corinthia deleted all of the pictures and continued down the other side of the hill.

When she was once again submerged in the maze, niches appeared in the underbrush, revealing low cactuses with pink fruits and four-inch spines. Mint-green snowballs of moss covered the ground. Delicate white flowers bloomed on branches with sage-shaped leaves.

It was so pretty, in its alien way, that Corinthia had almost relaxed when a sandpapery whisper rose somewhere behind her.

Corinthia turned, shades of ancestral caution already quickening her heartbeat, hands suddenly slick with sweat and automatically re-gripping the staff in a defensive pose.

A silvery snake surged out of the brush. It stopped in the center of the path. It flicked its tongue at Corinthia, once, twice, its eyes round and shining like glass beads.

Corinthia turned and ran. Her body, so comfortable sitting at the circulation desk or rolling out the free book cart, suddenly didn't seem to be properly designed for fleeing over soft sand, and especially not uphill. Her breath burned, her legs ached, and her feet seemed weighed down as if it were all a bad dream and unreality had an unfair advantage.

Suddenly the maze walls opened up, and there was a stand of full-sized pine trees and a completely improbable pond surrounded by low palmettos, as if a scrap of wetland had been cut-and-pasted into the maze.

Corinthia stopped. Tried to catch her breath. Tried to make sense of the pond. How could there be a pond in a place where water normally disappeared into the sand? The water in the ponds and lakes of Shadow Ridge usually looked like over-brewed black tea, but this pond was semi-transparent. Instead of being surrounded by a foot of muck and rot, the grass was dry right up to the edge of the water. It must have been recently rain-filled, Corinthia realized, and would probably disappear in a long dry spell.

Nearby, a collection of cut logs had been arranged. Corinthia made her way over to the logs and sat on a stump, then carefully set down the staff and looked at the map again.

The elevated pond was one of two ponds, one large and one small, both of which were marked *Ephemeral Wetland*. The smaller pond had a spot next to it marked *Woodland Theater*. This, she realized, was her current location. She glanced down at the log she was sitting on. It was very firm, compared to most theater seats.

Now that she knew where she was, she had not gone as far as she thought. She had traveled less than a quarter of the distance that stretched between the library, at the north end of the Refuge, and her backyard, at the south end. The highest point in the Refuge still lay ahead.

A harsh, scolding cry sounded from the top of a tree at the edge of the miniature wetland, and a flash of blue and silver gave away the position of a bird standing sentry on a high branch. *Attention, fellow birds! Here is a human intruder!*

Corinthia knew, from Stevie, that this bird was endangered—that it was why the Refuge was considered special—but had never understood, until that moment, why Stevie or anyone else had been so affected by sighting one of the rare scrub jays.

Its feathers were *so blue*. Like the Refuge itself, photos did not do it justice. Corinthia had never seen a blue like it. It wasn't robin blue or peacock blue. It was the color of a swimming pool when she finally worked up the courage to jump off the diving board. Blue like the frosting swirls on her twelfth birthday cake. Blue like her first crush's glittery eyeshadow.

Corinthia stood, pine straw crackling underfoot, and crept closer, one foot after another, slowly and carefully.

The scrub jay watched her approach with a jet-black eye—and then took off with an elegant glide. It swooped into the brush, lost to sight, and Corinthia was stood up like a prom date.

3

Though there was no sign of a snake on the walk back to the library, cries of "Kweep!" from unseen birds followed her all the way to the end of the trail.

Her little car waited in the parking lot. Corinthia climbed in gratefully, letting its worn but familiar interior wrap her in quiet isolation from the strangeness of the Refuge. The hike already felt like a dream, a dream that had happened to someone else entirely, someone she had left behind in the maze. Now she was herself again: well-ordered Corinthia, librarian, indoor person.

The car chugged jauntily out of the parking lot. A turn brought her onto the main road that ran alongside the Refuge. Corinthia found it oddly difficult to believe she had been walking around inside it. It seemed as remote as the surface of the moon.

Another turn and she sailed down the residential street bordering the south edge of the Refuge. The neighborhood had been built in the sixties for retirees from up north, and all of the houses were simple concrete block construction, rather like shoeboxes with pitched lids.

With no homeowner's association around to make rules, residents had taken it upon themselves to individualize the houses however they saw fit: collections of concrete statuary, year-round Christmas lights, and exterior paint colors that would have had Andy Warhol in raptures.

The original retirees were long gone, replaced by an assortment of residents as colorful as the houses. Young and old, with children or without, of many languages, they had only one thing in common: budgets that stretched just enough to buy a small house, but only in a place as unpretentious as Shadow Ridge.

Corinthia had kept the original paint on her home, mostly because it was too expensive to redo, and as such it remained Kelly green with dark emerald trim; or, as she liked to think of it, *Lucky Charms* chic, after the leprechaun on the cereal box.

She hurried to the door. Tonight was Halloween, and there was much to do before the trick-or-treaters arrived.

The first word anyone would have used to describe the inside of Corinthia's house was "small." The front door swung open directly into the living room. Within three strides you could be in the master bedroom; four strides, in the kitchen; five, in the tiny second bedroom on the other side of the house. It was almost ship-like in its coziness. Corinthia kept it ordered, as well, for she could not abide too much clutter.

There was a couch for lounging, a wing-back chair for reading, and a papasan chair for when Corinthia wanted to feel like she was curled up in a nest. If you looked closely, none of the furniture actually matched, but with enough soft pillows and blankets strewn about, the mix of colors blended together into something quite pleasing, like spilled paint accidentally making art.

There were no side tables, only small bookcases, and on top of the bookcases sat tabletop bookshelves, added later, to hold even more books.

Old coffee mugs sat here and there, occasionally holding a pen or pencil, but mostly holding dozens of various bookmarks. There was a bookshelf in the kitchen, too, and not even for cookbooks.

Books lay here and there like Easter eggs ready to be found: one on the floor, halfway under the sofa; one on the kitchen table; two fighting for space on the coffee table.

This did not take into account the bathroom book rack, the pile on Corinthia's nightstand, or the half dozen books sitting unbuckled in the back of her car.

Books were just... everywhere. And if you'd asked Corinthia if she should have perhaps had less books, she would have given you a stern look.

She was proud of what she had made of the old place, and had grown to not mind so much that the kitchen cabinets were falling apart. Stevie was her only visitor, and if Stevie didn't mind, then no one else of worth would mind either.

Sitting in the entryway was a dog with floppy velvet ears, short tricolor coat, and the most soulful eyes ever seen in a hound: Beaufort, a beagle and basset hound mix, who was quite possibly the world's most amiable canine.

"Beaufort," Corinthia said, with a formal tone, shutting the door behind her. "And how have you been this fine day?"

Beaufort trotted forward, tail wagging, eyes turned upward to his beloved mistress in an unashamed plea for pats, and preferably treats, too. Once in range he commenced sniffing his owner with such vigor that Corinthia couldn't take a single step forward for all the snuffling taking place.

Beaufort was the kind of dog who stood on two legs and put his front paws on you, not to wrestle you, but to stand tall enough to look into your eyes with a depth of genuine concern you might only expect from your mother. His eyes asked whether you'd eaten well and slept enough, and if you perhaps needed a hug. For Beaufort was a hugging dog: if you situated yourself on the couch, for example, he would place one front paw on each of your shoulders as if he'd known and loved you for years, even if you were only there to fix a sink. There was no creature on Earth who loved as truly, and with as much faith in humanity, as Beaufort.

Corinthia was unsure how a creature's eyes could appear to contain all the wisdom of the ages while that very same creature could be a complete and utter noodlehead, but Beaufort managed it. He was both thoughtful and silly, peaceful and playful, full of energy and content to curl up, nose-to-tail, in epic naps that lasted throughout whole afternoons.

"I've been on an adventure," Corinthia said, smoothing back Beaufort's ears. "But that's all done now, my friend. Sniff while you can—I won't be going back in there," she finished, patting the dog's smooth, spotted flank.

Beaufort sneezed, as if in disbelief.

Corinthia collared and leashed him for their regular after-work walk. There was something so wonderfully tame about walking through the neighborhood. While Beaufort could sniff and romp on the grass, Corinthia could keep her sneakers firmly on the relatively smooth and steady asphalt.

The sky was accessibly bright and blue, the trees generous with their leafy tambourines, and an assortment of common birds provided musical accompaniment, all without having to venture into any setting too wild, uncouth, or unruly. These were all separate qualities, and Corinthia relished each descriptor with intention, as if she were tasting different percentages of chocolate.

Now that she had seen the birds in the Refuge, she could not stop trying to distinguish the ones on her walk with Beaufort. The birds with the curved beaks, marching in loose formation across the lawn, were ibises. Those were easy. Other common birds she also recognized by sight—blue jay, cardinal, mockingbird, crow—but she had never quite gotten the knack of identifying them by song.

She downloaded the bird identification app Stevie was always going on about and waved her phone through the air like a butterfly net for catching songs. It lit up with one bird after another; some she had known about, but others she had never realized were hiding nearby: chickadees, chimney swifts, wrens, and more. And what was the bird of prey that sounded like it was saying "Uh-oh!" repeatedly from its perch on top of the telephone pole? Even the app didn't know.

Corinthia glanced at Beaufort. He didn't seem to pay much attention to avians unless they managed to flap into visual range. "Some help you are," she said.

Beaufort ambled on, unbothered.

When they returned, she changed into a Halloween sweater and emptied several bags of candy into a large plastic bowl. Although she had no particular like or dislike of children, viewing them simply as small versions of full-sized library patrons, she had strong feelings about what was owed to the community. As such, she felt duty-bound to be prepared with holiday-appropriate attire and a generous supply of individually-wrapped treats.

The sun set in a sky striped with shades of saltwater taffy pink, and a blanket of cool darkness fell over the street. The original builders had not seen fit to install streetlights—another cost-saving measure—but on Halloween night, though perhaps it took away from safety, it added to the atmosphere.

Corinthia turned on the front porch light to indicate she was open for the night's business, feeling strangely aware of the dark forest behind her home, beyond the back fence. Even in the warmth and light of the kitchen Corinthia felt the shades of long-lost trees rising from the cold sand below the foundation.

There was a knock at the door.

"Candy!" cried Corinthia, straightening her sweater and dashing to the table for the candy bowl. Beaufort perked up, his tail whipping nearly in circles with all the excitement, and followed Corinthia to the door. "Beaufort, stay," Corinthia said, raising a warning finger. The dog barked once, out of sheer elation, then settled into a sit.

Corinthia opened the door.

"Trick-or-treat!" A handful of children waved pillowcases and pumpkin buckets at her while their parents hung back in the driveway, watching proudly.

"Oh, my," Corinthia said, marveling at their costumes as she dropped exactly two pieces of candy in each bag or bucket. She could identify almost every character from a comic or TV or the movies, because they had all been made into picture books or graphic novels, and therefore had passed through her hands at the circulation desk a thousand times.

"Thank you!" they chorused, after being reminded by their parents.

Beaufort, unwilling to be left out, bayed the hound version of *You're welcome*: AWRH-roo AWRH-roo AWRH-roo.

Corinthia waved goodbye and closed the door, feeling very civic. Beaufort ran to the living room window and watched the children go.

They repeated this routine until the hour was reached when, by an unspoken agreement of unknown origin, each of the neighbors began to turn off their front porch lights. Corinthia popped a miniature chocolate bar into her mouth and went to do the same.

When her fingers landed on the switch, another knock came at the door.

It would have been rude to switch off the light while someone was standing on the doorstep, so Corinthia drew back her hand, hastily swallowed the chocolate, and opened the door.

4

There, on the front porch, stood Rosemary. Earlier that day, she had been wearing a fluttery blue and silver-gray dress, topped with a jeweled headpiece. Now she wore an elegant jumpsuit of the same material, a silky ombre of blue blended into silver-gray, cinched at the waist with a jeweled buckle.

Had she changed her entire outfit since the morning? If it had not been Halloween, Corinthia would have thought it extremely odd. It was almost like one of those as-seen-on-TV products she'd seen as a child: the traveling wardrobe, made of a handful of pieces that could be reversed, rearranged, or re-tied to create a dozen different outfits.

Corinthia hastily wiped her lips with the back of her hand, hoping to catch any remaining chocolate. "Hello... Rosemary, was it?" Corinthia knew the woman's name—would never have forgotten it as long as she lived, not even as an old, white-haired lady tucked under an afghan—but clung to a falsehood of unconcern like it was any protection at all against the fine, root-like filaments of tender feelings that were beginning to lace themselves into her heart.

Rosemary was beaming. "And you're Corinthia!"

"That's me," Corinthia admitted. An awkward silence stretched between them like caramel in a Halloween candy. This was the first time she had had a library patron show up at her home, and Corinthia didn't know whether to offer her a treat, like any other trick-or-treater; or invite her in; or simply shut the door in utter confusion—but Beaufort, who had been sitting a few feet back from the door, seized the moment and rushed forward.

He bounded past Corinthia and began sniffing around Rosemary's feet like he'd never sniffed such a fascinating person in his life.

"Beaufort! Get back here this instant," Corinthia said.

Beaufort did not, in fact, get back there that instant. He galloped in circles around Rosemary's ankles, stopping for a moment to sniff, and then taking off again, leading Corinthia round and round in a merry chase around the visitor.

Rosemary, for her part, ended up turning and turning to follow the action, and as a consequence the visitor and the librarian blundered into each other as the dog hopped out of the way, delighted at the fuss.

"Oh!" Rosemary cried, more in surprise than hurt.

"I am *so* sorry," Corinthia said, steadying Rosemary before dodging quickly to scoop up Beaufort, the trouble-causing hound.

Beaufort didn't make it easy, either, in that magical way he had of suddenly becoming twice as heavy. "Come along, you recalcitrant beast," she said to the dog. To Rosemary, she said, "Would you like to come inside?" because she felt a duty to make up for Beaufort's forwardness. "Please," she added. "Come in."

Rosemary's smile returned, and she glided over the threshold.

Corinthia, still holding the weighty dog, shut the door with her foot.

"Candy!" Rosemary cried, sweeping over to the bowl. She snagged a miniature chocolate bar, unwrapped it, and stuffed it neatly into her mouth like it was a piece of the finest sushi.

And what, Corinthia wondered, was the proper procedure when a visiting patron began helping herself to Halloween candy?

Beaufort's tongue lolled as he tilted his head to look at Rosemary quizzically, as if he, too, was trying to figure it out.

"Oh!" said Rosemary, after swallowing. "Shame on me. I have no manners whatsoever." Her graceful hands fluttered over the silk jumpsuit. One hand disappeared into a hidden pocket, then reappeared, holding a small, folded object.

Corinthia's wallet.

It lay on Rosemary's upturned palm, the worn leather shiny and smooth against the lines of her skin.

Beaufort strained toward the wallet, his twitching nose leading the way.

"I found it," Rosemary said. "In the Refuge."

Corinthia took the wallet, unable to avoid brushing her fingertips against the skin of Rosemary's palm, which was dry but firm, and lightly textured in the way of hands above a certain age. She held the wallet and tried to picture Rosemary, billowing silk and all, in the tangled maze of the Refuge, and could only imagine her floating, goddess-like, above it—as she herself, startled by a snake, blundered through in a panic until her wallet wiggled free and landed on the white sand, abandoned to its fate.

"I found your address on the card inside."

Corinthia looked up. "Card?"

Rosemary hesitated so briefly that the pause could have been an errant heartbeat and not a pause at all. "Your driver's license."

"Well," Corinthia said, returning the wallet to her pocket, unable to think of anything more scintillating. Bringing the wallet to her house was very like something she herself would have done, if she had found a driver's license. She often surprised others with her ways, so it was oddly pleasing that Rosemary had acted in a similar fashion. "Well!" Even Beaufort seemed to be waiting for her to say something more substantial. She set him down on the floor with a warning glance: *Behave.*

He sat as if he'd been behaving his whole life, tongue still lolling, gaze switching back and forth between Corinthia and Rosemary.

"Please, have all the candy you like," Corinthia said, feeling that it was a small price to pay for a returned valuable. Then, realizing this might be a childish thing to offer: "Or something to drink?"

"Oh, yes, please!" Rosemary picked up the candy bucket from the entryway table, and, with it tucked in the crook of one arm, swanned past Corinthia into the kitchen. She began opening all the cabinets without re-closing them.

And then Rosemary stumbled upon Corinthia's very special cabinet. "You have a whole cabinet," she said, her voice hushed with awe, "for chocolate?"

Corinthia did not drink, did not play the lottery, did not compulsively shop. When she had a little money she bought books, and if there was any left, she bought chocolate.

Corinthia did not consider the Cabinet of Chocolate a vice. It was more like a medicine cabinet full of healthful cocoa products. At its most recent inventory it contained two tins of Guittard Cocoa Rouge; eight different flavors of chocolate bars including milk chocolate, white chocolate, dark chocolate, 90% chocolate, and a handful of flavored bars; an unopened bottle of the all-natural version of Hershey's Chocolate Syrup (the opened one was in the fridge); a box of truffles, lined with gold tissue; and, for those late-night sweet-and-salty insomnia cravings, a bag of chocolate-covered pretzels.

Corinthia, who had been about to reassert control over the situation, relented. She joined Rosemary at the Cabinet of Chocolate, too proud of it to close it up and stop the admiration.

Rosemary had pulled down a tin of Cocoa Rouge. She opened the lid and stuck her nose inside, inhaling with little sniffs. "I've read you should do this," she said, still nose-deep in the cocoa tin, "rather than take really big sniffs. That it works better for smelling something lovely and delicate." Her dark and shining gaze lifted to Corinthia's.

Corinthia swallowed. "Definitely," she said, helplessly pleased by the attention to her fine selection of chocolate and also unnerved by the intrusion. When she took the tin away their fingers touched again and Corinthia's brain short-circuited like a misbehaving laser printer. "Do you spend a lot of time in the Refuge?"

"Positively ages," Rosemary said, taking down the chocolate bars one by one and examining them up close.

"In that dress you were wearing earlier?"

"Why not?" Rosemary tore open the milk chocolate and took a bite.

Not knowing what else to say, Corinthia asked if she liked it.

"Mmm," Rosemary said, with so much relish her eyes closed and she swayed on her feet.

Corinthia opened the dark chocolate bar and wordlessly handed it over, watching as Rosemary bit into it eagerly, as if she'd been marooned on a desert island for years, without chocolate. Perhaps she had been on a low-carb diet and couldn't help herself.

Indeed she did help herself, to the truffles and the chocolate-covered pretzels, all the while making exclamations of pleasure and satisfaction.

Beaufort, who seemed to have determined that the stranger was unusual but not a threat, retreated to his dog bed, turned around three times, and then settled with his head on his paws, watching Rosemary and Corinthia do the strange, inexplicable things humans did.

"How about some hot cocoa?" Corinthia finally said, hoping to slow down the sugar rampage Rosemary was committing upon the Cabinet of Chocolate. "I make my own bedtime blend."

Rosemary stopped just as she was about to rip the seal off the chocolate syrup, seeming to catch herself in mid-tear. She set down the bottle and covered her mouth briefly, her eyes wide. "I am so sorry," she said. "I don't know what came over me. It's all so good I couldn't stop myself."

Corinthia's pride in her chocolate selections overcame her initial shock at having her cabinet ransacked. "It's all right," she said. "Sometimes I do the same thing." She offered Rosemary the rest of the truffles to nibble while the milk heated in the saucepot, then added her own blend of dried herbs and flowers—chamomile, spearmint, lemongrass, tilia flowers, hawthorn, and rosebuds—to steep.

Rosemary watched with interest. "Do you have trouble sleeping?"

"Sometimes." The word left out the truth of the dark, quiet nights, unpredictable in their attack, that left her unable to sleep until the first light of the sun made her eyelids heavy at last.

"I could help you," Rosemary said. "I have a knack."

Corinthia chuckled, ready to good-naturedly humor this pretty woman with her silk and her funny ways, though she believed in nothing that smacked of the new-age. "Cocoa first," she said. "Then you can cure my insomnia and I'll go right to bed, like a good girl."

Steam rose and the air filled with fragrance. Corinthia strained the milk, slowly blended the cocoa powder, and then carefully poured the cocoa into two cups.

The cups were small and they finished it standing right there in the kitchen. When Corinthia was done, she placed the cup back in its saucer with a decisive clink, like a bell ringing *time's up*.

Rosemary set hers down as well, only this time the sound dinged the timer starting again. They weren't finished yet, it seemed to say. Rosemary gestured: *come closer*.

"You're not going to bean me with a frying pan, are you?"

"I'm going to massage your temples," Rosemary said, her voice matter-of-fact.

Corinthia didn't normally like to be touched by strangers, but she knew Rosemary's name and Rosemary had complimented her Cabinet of Chocolate and they both approved of *Alien Space Lesbians*, and now they couldn't be considered strangers, could they? On top of that, it had been a rather long time since she had been touched at all. Perhaps it was the influence of the Halloween moon, but this overture seemed like a treat and not a trick.

And so, by the time she came out of her thoughts long enough to realize that Rosemary's fingertips were already brushing her temples, Corinthia did not pull away.

"Close your eyes," Rosemary said.

All was dark save for the afterimages of the kitchen lights. The scent of the chocolate and flowers and herbs softly perfumed the air. Corinthia breathed in as Rosemary's firm fingertips stroked her temples, causing the hair on the back of her neck to rise. No one had touched her like this in so long that it came as quite a shock, almost literally electric as tiny pinpricks tickled her scalp like static. It would have been unseemly to sigh as the pleasure of almost uncontrollable relaxation rolled through her like a warm, deep ocean wave, so Corinthia held her breath for a moment instead.

"All done," Rosemary said. She pressed a fingertip to the end of Corinthia's nose and wiggled it, teasingly. "You can open your eyes."

Corinthia obeyed, slightly scandalized by the nose-booping. "Is that it?"

"That's it."

"Will I fall asleep now?"

"Lie down and find out."

Corinthia realized that half of the remaining candy had disappeared from the bowl, and could not fathom how that might have happened, short of patting down Rosemary's hidden pockets. "Thank you for finding my wallet," she said.

"Thank you for losing it," Rosemary replied, moving toward the door, possibly with half the contents of the candy bowl. "I wish you beautiful dreams."

They were at the door.

"I wish you..." Corinthia paused, unsure of how to finish this unusual parting. Then, as she opened the front door, she thought of the book Rosemary had taken. "I hope you enjoy the romance."

"I certainly do," Rosemary replied. With that, she kissed her own fingertips and blew the kiss across the threshold to Corinthia, then turned and was gone from sight.

Corinthia closed the door.

Beaufort roused himself and loped to the front window, looking left and right, before finally letting out a disconsolate howl.

Corinthia looked out the front window. There was no one to be seen.

Rosemary was already gone.

Corinthia led Beaufort away from his post and then let him into the fenced backyard. Occasionally this meant shooing him away from howling at squirrels or birds, but even if he had let out a howl or two, it would have been all right because her neighbors on all sides ascribed to a sort of unspoken, reciprocal noninterference pact which would have made the United Nations proud.

After luring Beaufort inside with a tiny nibble of chicken, Corinthia dropped heavily onto the couch, unsure of what to make of any of it.

She finally settled for lying all the way down while picturing Rosemary's clever face and mysterious eyes. There were things to do before bedtime—things to be tidied or ordered; taken out or put away—and yet Corinthia did none of them. Instead she was already composing the story for Stevie, imagining how Stevie would laugh at the idea of Rosemary rubbing Corinthia's temples; the kiss that winged its way across the threshold; how Stevie would ask if it really worked, and how Corinthia would shake her head with a smile, because: *of course it didn't.*

All of this washed out like a wave receding, leaving behind a sense of being covered by warm, dry sand, cozy and heavy. Then the wave returned, turning everything to darkness and moon-haloed clouds and distant stars, and there was no sense of danger, only peace, as Corinthia went quietly under the tide of sleep.

5

Upon waking the following morning to the sound of Beaufort pawing at the back door, Corinthia bolted upright from a vivid dream of flying over the Refuge. She had never meant to fall asleep on the couch, and everything that had felt so easy and comfortable the night before now felt like a massive error in judgment.

A stranger! Inside her own little house, decimating her Cabinet of Chocolate, using some kind of silly mumbo jumbo and ignoring Corinthia's carefully guarded personal space.

It seemed like a good idea at the time, Corinthia of the previous night whispered, ghostlike, in her memory.

"Nonsense," Corinthia said aloud.

After taking care of Beaufort and getting her own personal appearance into some semblance of order, Corinthia left for the library. Instead of waiting for Stevie to intrude upon the sacred circulation desk, Corinthia marched into the environmental center, right past the taxidermied hawk, who seemed especially surprised to see her.

"Stevie!"

Stevie whirled around from where she had been feeding the turtles and the baby alligators. "Christ on a cracker, woman! You scared me."

The story tumbled out: Halloween, trick-or-treat, Rosemary on the doorstep, the dog's odd reaction, the chocolate, the scalp massage, their goodbyes. *Sleep.*

Corinthia finished the story and waited for laughter to come like a lash, a fitting punishment for her foolishness.

Instead, Stevie's mouth had fallen open. The aquariums burbled in the background. Finally, she said, with the air of the amazed: "Whoa..."

"*Whoa*?" Corinthia said. "What do you mean, 'whoa'? I let a stranger come into my house and touch my—my *person*—and got so bedazzled I passed out on the couch, and all you can say is, 'Whoa'?"

Finally, Stevie laughed. Then she threw her arm around her friend. "I'm proud of you, Corinthia." Stevie gave her a little shake. "You actually did something fun for once."

Corinthia extricated herself, crossed her arms, and turned away. She watched a turtle lazily propel itself through the water. "I don't even remember dropping my wallet."

"Why would you? You were running from a snake!"

"What if that woman stole it?"

Stevie scoffed. "*Stole* it. Right. She sidled up to you in the Refuge, picked your pocket like the Artful Dodger, and disappeared. And all of this without you noticing a thing."

Corinthia paced in front of the hawk, whose head didn't move, but the light reflected in its glass eyes made it appear that its gaze followed her anyway. "I walked *back* the same way I walked *in*. I would have *seen* my wallet if it fell out."

"You're overthinking this." *Like you overthink everything,* Stevie didn't have to say. "If some beautiful woman brought me back my lost wallet—heck, maybe even if she stole it in the first place—and then went into ecstasies over the contents of one of my kitchen cabinets and massaged my head and gave me the best night of my life—"

"Best night of *sleep* of my life," Corinthia corrected.

"Whatever. I know what *I'd* do."

"What's that?" Corinthia said, suspiciously, half-expecting something inappropriate.

"Marry her."

This was too ridiculous to address, and therefore Corinthia did not address it. "I want to go back."

"Back where?"

"The Refuge."

"Why? You fulfilled your end of the bet. Why would you do that to yourself again? I mean, you don't even like the outdoors, *and* you got chased by a snake."

"I feel like I'm missing something."

"You were missing your wallet."

Corinthia shook her head, distractedly, as if to clear it. "I'm missing something," she repeated. Something was calling to her, and she didn't want to satisfy it but she also wanted it to stop. Then she could close the whole matter, like a book, and put it back on the shelf.

Stevie looked at her for a long moment. "I'll come with you."

Corinthia looked up. "You will?"

"What are friends for? Besides, I know more about the Refuge than you do."

Corinthia preferred to know the most about almost everything, but even she could admit that Stevie's expertise in this area was unquestioned. "Right after work," she said, unwilling—for reasons unknown even to herself—to delay by any but the smallest and most necessary amount.

"Right after work," Stevie agreed.

Back in the library, Corinthia refreshed the free book cart and collected the books from the bin beneath the return slot. *Alien Space Lesbians* was not there.

Where *was* that book, anyway?

The computer said it hadn't been checked out; that it was still on the shelf in the Shadow Ridge Library. Corinthia checked the new book display. She checked the regular fiction shelves. She scanned the carts of books pulled for repair. She even walked a circuit of all the tables to make doubly sure it hadn't been casually left out.

Nothing.

No one had checked it out. And no one could have simply walked out with it, either, because the radio frequency ID tag would have made the security system squawk. The simplest answer was that someone had left it somewhere, and she, Corinthia, couldn't possibly have covered every possible square inch where it might have been misplaced.

Yes, that was almost certainly correct.

With correctness usually came peace, but Corinthia spent the rest of the workday in a fog of unease, all thumbs, and when she fumbled a book she was carrying, it fell and struck the lowest metal shelf like a gong.

What had seemed like a good idea in the morning became less so in the afternoon. Corinthia faced the trailhead with Stevie, who was fairly bouncing with excitement.

"I never thought you'd want to come out here with me," Stevie enthused. "I thought you'd always want to stay inside, comfy old Corinthia, with your books and your dog and your blankets—"

"Thank you for making me sound one hundred years old."

"And here you are!"

"Here I am," Corinthia said, eyeing the trail ahead and wondering, not for the first time, what had possessed her. She could have turned back just then, forgotten the whole thing; except she couldn't have forgotten. Something about the place clung to her, wouldn't let her go, wouldn't let her stop thinking about white sand and tangled green trees and blue-and-silver-winged birds.

"Shall we go?" Stevie prompted.

Corinthia patted her wallet through the outside of her pocket, and then nodded to Stevie to lead the way. On this, the windiest day she had ever been in the Refuge, the breeze sounded not like wind but like the roar of the ocean that, long ago, had surrounded this place.

Stevie kept up a steady patter of facts, identifying many of the plants by sight: "That's horsemint—blooms during spring and summer, mostly," or "That's a staggerbush," or "Watch out for prickly pear spines!" Corinthia learned that there were four kinds of oak in the Refuge (Chapman's, turkey, myrtle, and sand live oak), and that the puffy gray-green snowballs were deer lichen, often incorrectly referred to as deer moss.

Normally Stevie's chatter would have soothed Corinthia. As someone who spoke less, Corinthia found it easy to relax into the stream of someone else's words, provided that they were interesting enough. But in the Refuge she found herself secretly wishing to hoard the place to herself, to hear only the whispers of her own footsteps in the sand.

Florida was prettier without houses. Corinthia felt the presence of her own, to the south, and felt slightly ashamed. There was nothing right about this at all and yet there it was.

Corinthia spoke even less than usual, only indicating the outbound path she'd taken so that Stevie retraced those steps. Stevie happily filled in the gaps: here was a shiny blueberry bush; there was a *Florida* rosemary bush, and that one over there was a *false* rosemary bush, neither of which were true culinary rosemary. The birds swooping overhead were a flock of swallows, visitors to the Refuge—unlike the scrub jays, who never left their small scrubland territory.

They came upon the spot where, in Corinthia's recollection, the snake had crossed her path. There were no snakes to be seen, but Stevie pointed out how the burrowing creatures had pushed up the lower layer of sand, leaving small heaps of golden yellow sand atop the white.

Corinthia paced the spot. She jumped up and down in an attempt to dislodge her wallet. She even jogged back and forth a few times, to Stevie's obvious amusement. By the end of it she had to admit it could have fallen out, especially since she'd run much farther in her flight from the snake, and that because there were so many criss-crossing trails, Rosemary could have found the wallet, disappeared into any of a dozen trails, and exited the Refuge without ever being seen.

Stevie had crossed her arms while waiting. "Satisfied?"

Corinthia said nothing but took the lead.

They passed the Ephemeral Wetland and the Woodland Theater. They hiked up the highest hill, which was topped with pine trees, and descended again into the maze of oaks. All the while the birds talked in their own chirpy language, sounding—to Corinthia's burning ears—like a flock of shameless gossips.

There was a scruffy scrub jay in the bush to the side of the trail, watching her. If it had been a human, it would have had a wrinkled face and a worried expression. Instead of jaunty chirps, this one murmured softly, as if nervously asking a question.

They walked on. When they next stopped to drink water, Corinthia spotted something deep in the shadows of the oak scrub: a whorl of twigs formed into a bowl-like shape, sitting just at Corinthia's height.

"A nest," Stevie confirmed. "Nesting season is in the spring, though, so this is an old one."

"Do they use them over again?"

"Not typically."

Corinthia moved closer to the nest, carefully lifting oak branches out of the way when they threatened to tangle her hair, feeling extremely brave. Stevie's commentary reached her like a cheerful nature documentary: "There's an outer basket made of larger twigs and an inner basket made of smaller twigs and palm fibers. A nest within a nest."

Corinthia drew level with the nest and raised herself on her tiptoes to see inside.

She dropped back onto flat feet. What she saw simply wasn't possible.

"Stevie," she called. "Do they typically line the nest with books?"

"Books? No. Maybe a few strips from a lost page." Stevie laughed. "Just a few favorite quotes."

Corinthia went on tiptoe again. There, nestled snugly in the inner basket, were three books: a discarded selection of poems by Emily Dickinson, a discarded copy of *Woodworking and You*... and a book with a very purple, very scaled, space lesbian on the cover. "Stevie," she repeated. "Come look."

Stevie made her way through the twisted branches and joined Corinthia.

They peered into the abandoned nest—if it could be called abandoned, if it was being used as a sort of woodland bookshelf.

"Who put those there?" Stevie said.

"You tell me." Corinthia gingerly reached into the nest and withdrew the sci-fi romance. She examined it with a librarian's eye: no water damage, no spine cracking, no dog-eared pages. With the exception of a dried leaf inserted at the end of chapter three—a bookmark?—it was as well-cared for as if it had stayed in the library.

Part of her wanted to put it back in the nest. The librarian part did not.

"Should we take the other two as well?" Stevie asked.

"Hmm?" Corinthia glanced up at the volumes of poetry and woodworking. "Well, they *were* on the free book cart." She should know, because she put them there with her own two hands.

"The scrub jays certainly aren't going to read them," Stevie joked.

"No, of course not," Corinthia said. She hugged the romance to her chest, where her heart beat against the cover, faster than the hike would have justified. "If they're still there in a few days, I'll collect them and put them back on the free book cart."

"So you're coming out here again?"

"Someone has to."

"Why not just take them now?"

Corinthia had reasons; good reasons, she was sure. She just couldn't think of what they were. "They'll be fine," she said, like the discarded books were children who were old enough to wander the neighborhood alone.

They walked back toward the Shadow Ridge Library, and Stevie picked up her happy lecture about scrubland ecology with a tangent on the renewing effects of fire and hurricanes.

When the walls of the green maze closed tighter, there was a rustle from within followed by a burst of blue movement.

A scrub jay landed in front of them on the white sand path.

Stevie stopped, and Corinthia stopped, and the scrub jay looked up at them with a shrewdly observant eye. It hopped forward boldly, examining the intruders—visitors? How did it view them?

"It's probably looking for acorns," Stevie said. "Acorns are their favorite food. They bury thousands of them in the sand."

Stevie was closer but the scrub jay hopped past her to Corinthia, who wanted to backpedal but didn't, for fear of scaring it.

A startling beating of wings, a rush of air, and a weight dropped onto Corinthia's head with sharp pinpricks holding it in place. "Stevie," she said, carefully, "is there a bird on my head?"

Stevie was staring at her, open-mouthed. "Don't move!" She rummaged for her phone.

"Stevie," Corinthia added, "if you take a photograph of this I will bury your body beneath six feet of white sand."

"Don't be such a grump," Stevie said, cheerfully ignoring the threat and snapping the photo. "There! It wants your book, see?" She turned the phone screen around to display it.

Whack. The bird knocked Corinthia square in the head with its sharp, strong beak.

"Ow!" Corinthia resisted the urge to swat the beautiful, personal space-invading bird away.

"Aw, it likes you," Stevie said.

"It most certainly does not." The bird shuffled its feet and more gently plucked at Corinthia's hair, as if apologizing. Or considering lining its nest. "Go on, bird," she said. "Go home."

The weight of the bird increased for a moment then lifted away entirely as the bird flew to a nearby branch. It looked at Corinthia reproachfully, as if to say, *I am home*, before disappearing into the oak branches.

6

After their short jaunt into the Refuge, Corinthia and Stevie headed to the parking lot for the weekly pop-up market of food trucks and local vendors.

They stopped a few yards from Drew's D-Lites, their planned dinner destination. Kitschy Florida art covered the outside of the vehicle: painted palm trees, surfboards, alligators, and flamingos, plus a few oranges and mermaids for good measure. Inside, Drew was wearing an open Hawaiian-print shirt over her black tank top, along with Ray-Bans and a Panama hat, because Drew was fully committed to the bit.

Corinthia nudged Stevie. "Go on."

Stevie didn't move.

"Just *talk* to her."

Stevie shook out her hands in a spasm of nervous energy. "I can't."

"You were both flirting with each other yesterday!"

"But what if she was just being *polite*?"

"Ask her if she'd like to join a book club for two." Corinthia gave Stevie a push to get her moving.

They approached the food truck counter.

Drew slung a kitchen towel over her shoulder and greeted them both with a smile. "What can I get you ladies today?"

Stevie, who had gone entirely mute, nudged Corinthia.

Corinthia eyed the menu board with great seriousness. There were only a few menu items, but she gave them proper deliberation as if they were engraved on linen paper, in French, at the finest restaurant. In a way, they were just as inscrutable, with names like The Devil Dog, The Pickle Pooch, and The Drewburger. The Orange Drew was Drew's version of an Orange Julius: fresh-squeezed orange juice, milk, real vanilla, and a hint of egg for froth.

"We'll have two Devil Dogs and two Orange Drews, please."

"Two Devil Dogs and two Orange Drews, coming up." She slapped the counter for emphasis, then turned away to work the machinery.

"You were supposed to say something," Corinthia murmured to Stevie.

"I got nervous."

Corinthia sighed. Surrounded by the reassuring brick and mortar of civilization, waiting for a bounty of Drew's D-Lites, she had a strange impulse to bulldoze it all; let it fall; roll out the quilt of the Refuge as far as the eye could see, all of Shadow Ridge carpeted over, even the library a heap of broken shelves and aged paper, a tattered copy of *Lolly Willowes* the only readable text left under a roof cracked open to the sky.

When their order was ready, they collected it, and Corinthia had almost turned away when she remembered to ask: "Have you seen a woman dressed all in blue out here today?"

"Blue? Blue..." Drew leaned on the counter and cocked her head. "Not that I recall. Only a pretty lady in a blue t-shirt," she added, and tipped her hat at Stevie.

Stevie glanced down at her own t-shirt, only just realizing it was blue, then looked back up with a grin.

They collected their Devil Dogs and drinks and walked on.

It took some juggling to handle the hot dog and the cup, but Corinthia managed. The bun was pillow-soft; the hot dog was just the right temperature, with the perfect snap; and the mustard was spicy enough to keep it interesting.

Corinthia drank the frothy, creamy orange beverage until her stomach shivered with cold. A new hunger made it tastier, more satisfying, and Corinthia had no explanation for where this appreciation came from, only that it felt as if something was waking up for the first time.

There were sellers of candles, and crocheted stuffed animals, and local authors with books stacked high; kitschy wreaths and cutting boards and homemade dog biscuits; lotions and soaps and every variety of baked good and fried snack. They wandered until Stevie spotted her favorite tent and, after depositing their trash in a nearby bin, she dragged Corinthia into it.

"Oh, no, not this one again," Corinthia said.

"Stop being a killjoy," Stevie retorted.

The tables beneath the tent were piled high with packs of tarot cards, baskets of colored stones, packets of incense, and bottles of essential oil. Stevie immediately began examining tall pillar candles, reading aloud their supposed magical powers: "'Magic Money.' 'Bad Spell Remover.' 'Come to Me.' Ooh, that one sounds good for you. You can find the mystery lady." She held it out to Corinthia, who took it and placed it decisively back on the table. Undaunted, Stevie plucked a crystal out of a basket instead. "This one's for mental focus—"

"Get that one," Corinthia said, dryly.

"Very funny." She picked up a bloodstone, dark green and flecked with red. "For abundance."

"If they sell enough of them, yes."

Stevie brandished a blue stone. "Altered consciousness!"

"Unaltered consciousness is good enough for me."

"Moonstone! Isn't there just something magical about this one?" Stevie cupped the stone in her hand and let the light play across its pearlescent surface.

"What does that one do? Your taxes?"

Stevie used her free hand to shove Corinthia. "Intuition and wisdom, you stodgy old stick."

"Stevie," Corinthia said. "There is no such thing as magic. And if there *were* such a thing as magic, why would a rock dug out of a pit halfway across the world have literally any relevance whatsoever"—she swept her hand through the air—"here in Shadow Ridge?"

Stevie blinked down at the moonstone. "Are you saying it's not *local* enough?"

The vendor, who had been standing off to the side pretending not to hear their conversation, drifted a few feet closer.

Corinthia forged on nevertheless. "If—not that I *believe* this, mind you—but *if* there were such a thing as magic and *if* you could manipulate it in some way, it certainly wouldn't be with trinkets dug up wholesale." She picked up a pink quartz. "'Love,' it says. Why is that? Is it because it's pink? *Pink* for *love* is just a cheap cultural reference and a thoroughly new one, at that. I don't buy it."

The vendor was frowning, and Corinthia realized she was, in fact, on the border of killjoy territory.

"But I *will* buy this crystal," Corinthia rallied, handing it to the vendor, who looked genuinely startled.

"You will?" asked Stevie.

"Yes," Corinthia said. "Because it's a pretty color. And because it makes you happy. And if I don't believe in magic, well! I can still believe in happiness, can't I?" She paid the vendor and took the little paper bag, which crinkled with the sound of the tissue paper cradling the crystal inside, then handed the bag to a bemused Stevie.

"You're very strange, Corinthia," she said, as they walked away. "I could almost imagine you *do* believe in magic."

Corinthia harrumphed. "There's more magic in a handful of plain white sand than in that entire gaudy display." Strangely, she felt the presence of the sand beneath the asphalt: cold, locked down, and deep; and, more distantly, where it wound between the dense oak trees of the scrub, warm from the sun and tumbled by the wind. *Come back*, it said.

Corinthia brushed off her arms as if sand had dusted them.

"Are you going to return *Alien Space Lesbians*?" Stevie said, admiring the pink quartz she'd pulled out of the bag.

The book lay heavily in Corinthia's bag at that very moment. "Yes," she said. "Of course."

"You don't want to read it first?"

"I will when I get around to it," she said, with feigned nonchalance. She couldn't say that her desire to read the book burned like a fire. It was too much to share with anyone save perhaps Beaufort, who would not judge and would keep it to himself. Corinthia cast about for a way to change the subject, and, not being particularly adept at it, landed on a topic familiar to them both. "Have you ever gotten lost in the Refuge?" Corinthia asked.

"Only once," Stevie said.

"Only once? I'd have figured it was easy to get lost in there."

"It is, but when it happened, I'd been working there for five years. So it *shouldn't* have been easy."

"Wait a minute," Corinthia said. "You'd been running around in there for half a decade, and *then* you got lost? How is that even possible?"

"Well," Stevie said, "I don't rightly know. I was leading a group on the long trail, all the way to the bigger of the two Ephemeral Wetlands—we were a little over halfway there, I think—and all of a sudden I got turned around. Nothing looked familiar."

"But you can see landmarks from most of the big trails..."

"I know! I even had my phone, as a map. But the map didn't line up with the landmarks. Everything was just slightly off. As in, if I thought I was facing north, the map showed I was actually facing north-northeast. Or it might have even been the other way around. I don't know."

"What did you do?"

"I did the only thing I could do. I got to high ground, spotted the library building, and took everyone back. I couldn't risk running those people around in circles until I figured out where the Ephemeral Wetland had hidden itself. Very embarrassing."

"Why do you think you got lost?"

"Magic," Stevie said.

"Magic," Corinthia echoed, full of crystal-averse skepticism.

"Sure," Stevie replied. "Local magic. We don't have any crystals around here, so maybe it's in everything else."

"If everything is magic, then nothing is magic."

"Maybe it's that simple."

Corinthia raised her eyebrows and said nothing.

"Maybe everything *is* magic," Steve finished.

"*That's* your unified field theory?"

"I like it," Stevie said cheerfully.

Corinthia let it ride. Early evening sunlight poured over everything like melted butter, until even the plainest things were gilded, and Corinthia could almost—but not quite—admit that the world could be imagined as Stevie saw it.

Come back, the Refuge whispered.

Which was impossible, because Corinthia had most certainly not purchased a blue rock and entered an altered state of consciousness. The sweet taste of orange was fresh on her lips; the book bumped against her as she walked; even the quiet crunch of gravel underfoot conspired to keep her quite literally grounded. *No flights of fancy*, she reassured herself.

Upon parting from Stevie, it was reassuring to return home to Beaufort and the very earth-bound routine of patting, brushing, praising, and giving treats. Corinthia decided to take the longest route for Beaufort's walk, both for the dog's sheer joy and her own conviction that walking the neighborhood was a way of contributing to the overall good feelings of the community.

She leashed the hound and headed out the door, Beaufort's soulful eyes rolling upward to the heavens as the dog caroled a series of happy howls.

It was only a few houses down when Corinthia began to detect something about her street that she'd never noticed before. Having been used to thinking of the terrain as flat, she had smoothed out the hills, valleys, and ridges that actually existed, and now, like an illustration in a pop-up book, they suddenly sprang into existence. The street curved down, then up, then plateaued. Underneath the shoebox houses and asphalt roads, and the varying efforts at landscaping, it was the same up-and-down terrain as the Refuge.

Had a bulldozer just scraped everything away?

Did any original plants remain?

There were ornamental palm trees; citrus trees that had obviously been planted when the houses were built; and grass, grass everywhere. Even if it wasn't a true monoculture, considering that everyone seemed to collectively agree to let other short-growing plants run wild, the street looked like the Refuge had been painted out with asphalt and lawns.

Corinthia adored her little house; was grateful she had been able to find something so suitable; understood that the affordable homes were a lifeline not just for her but for the entire Shadow Ridge community; and yet, this was a sadness like no other.

So much had been lost. There were no scrub jays here, and the need to see one again struck Corinthia with sudden force.

In the distance, she could see the tallest trees that bordered the Refuge: pine trees that topped a high ridge, casting shadows as the sun inexorably set. It was too late to enter the Refuge. Dark would fall soon, and there were rules about when one could enter. Between sunrise and sunset, as Corinthia recalled.

Corinthia liked rules. They made life simpler.

So when she found herself, upon returning from the leisurely walk, selecting a light jacket least likely to snag on grasping branches, she was entirely surprised.

7

She brought the book. She didn't know why—only that it stayed in her bag, when it should have been removed to lighten the weight; when it had absolutely no chance of being read any time soon, especially not in the fading light.

Still she carried it when she entered the Refuge, when the buttery light had cooled to silver.

The knowledge that she shouldn't be there floated as distant as the cold-weather clouds, traced in the sky in the shape of horse tails. The sound of her sneakers striking the path drew her thoughts away from rule-breaking and hushed them with soothing whispers of sand.

Before, daylight had made the landscape stark in its strangeness. Now dusk blurred it until the walls of the maze became softened shadows, shifting their pathways when she looked away, like Castle Adventure and its movable walls.

The noises were different, too. Where before there were cries of hawks in flight, now there were quiet rustles of feathers in the deep brush, like small shaken-out blankets before bed. No snakes darted across the path this time, and if there were bees, they, too, had fallen silent. There were deep-voiced bullfrogs, and some other kind of frog, higher-pitched but cacophonous, with a sound like marbles crashing together in a bag.

The still-closed blooms on the lyonia bushes smelled like honey; the shorter brush to the sides of the trail smelled faintly of woodsmoke from old lightning strikes; every step turned up the salty scent of the beach; and below it all, rising from the aquifer deep beneath the sand, an exhalation of fresh, mineral-filled springwater.

The flashlight looked too bright. Corinthia turned it down until it was a soft circle of false moonlight, and then turned it off entirely. It was now truly dark.

It was against the rules to be in the Refuge after dark.

If it was against the rules, then why was she there? She should have rightfully returned the book to the shelf as her job required. Corinthia lived for rightful. How satisfying it would have been, to file the book on its shelf, alphabetically by author. And yet she carried the book further down the path, away from the library, away from rules and rightfulness, further up and further into the Refuge, knowing it was something she *must* do.

The path curved onward into the stand of pine trees that outlined the Ephemeral Wetland. Corinthia smelled the water before she could see it: it was crisp and metallic like cooled tea. Perhaps she could leave the book on one of the stumps and wash her hands of it; the chance of finding the nest again, especially in the dark, was slim to none. Whoever had taken it in the first place would surely run across it before any rain came—even while breaking the rules, Corinthia could not bear to think of a book being damaged.

She stopped and took it out of her bag. When she looked up, a breeze had rippled the surface of the water in the distance, fracturing it like a mirror, each crack lined with white light.

The ripples flowed toward a toppled pine tree that Corinthia hadn't noticed before. Its trunk extended far out into the pond, like a bridge to nowhere ending in a puff of branches.

Only—it *wasn't* a puff of branches.

It was a person, sitting on the log, for all intents and purposes appearing to be intentionally perched in the most unlikely of places.

Rosemary.

She wore what appeared to be a silk pajama set, color indistinguishable in the dark, with contrasting piping, and jeweled buttons on the shirt that glittered with diamondesque flashes so crisp they could have made an audible sound, like chimes.

Pajamas. In the woods.

All at once she knew why she had been compelled to bring the book. The forest had called—the forest had brought them together—and Corinthia opened her mouth, for the first time in her life without thinking ahead, and called out: "I've brought you your book!"

Rosemary wobbled on her perch. Her arms flew outward for balance. The gemstone buttons on her shirt cast their twinkles chaotically, like tiny stars flung around the clearing, until Rosemary lost her balance completely and fell off the log with a ringing splash that sent water flying into the air.

Corinthia gasped, dropped the book and the bag, and ran for the water. Her footfalls landed, left-right, left-right, with the refrain of *your fault, your fault.*

"I'm sorry!" she cried, racing to where she'd seen Rosemary fall, heedless of possible snakes or thorns, her shoes an instant ruin in the tea-like water, the cold seizing her around the ankles like it would drag her in entirely, to be finished off by the grasping, gooey mud.

Rosemary surfaced, dripping water, the depth of the pond a thick swirl of ink below the moonlit surface.

Corinthia rushed to her, seized her by the arms, and drew her up. Water fell from Rosemary in sheets. "Are you okay?"

Rosemary held Corinthia's arms and said nothing for a moment, only gazed at her, dark eyes full of moonlight.

Corinthia, for whom feeling guilty was an infrequent but highly painful experience, began to ask *Are you okay?* again but did not get more than the first syllable out before Rosemary laid a cool, wet, silencing finger on Corinthia's lips.

Corinthia was shivering. Corinthia was in shock. Corinthia who would have normally shaken off such contact in an instant simply froze in place.

"You came back," Rosemary said. Her fingertip traced a curve from Corinthia's lips to Corinthia's jawline. "You brought the book," she added, with wonder, punctuating the statement with a soft tap on Corinthia's chin.

Corinthia, who had broken through the fence of known experiences and was now wandering, mentally, on the other side, nodded. Another shiver passed through her body. "We should—we should get you out of here. Get you some dry things. You must be freezing."

Corinthia was freezing, too, but hadn't actually noticed until that moment. Then all the sensations of cold rushed in at once: goosebumps, the heavy wet clothes, the weight in her shoes.

"Come," Rosemary said, slipping an arm around Corinthia's waist as if Corinthia was the one who truly needed help.

Belatedly, Corinthia remembered who was supposed to be the rescuer, and put her arm around the smaller woman's shoulders, and together they walked out of the Ephemeral Pond.

"We should get you home," Corinthia said, logic beginning to reassert itself.

"I am home," Rosemary said, giving Corinthia's waist a little squeeze. Did she mean the Refuge? Of course not—it made no sense.

Corinthia didn't know what to do, until Rosemary trembled. "Let's get you inside," Corinthia said. She collected her bag and the book, and tucked them under one arm, which was not quite as wet as her lower half. Then she wrapped her other arm around Rosemary, for warmth, and so joined they retraced Corinthia's path toward the library building.

"What were you doing out here so late?" Corinthia asked.

"What were *you* doing out here so late?" Rosemary countered.

"I wanted to see what it was like," Corinthia admitted. "After dark."

Rosemary chuckled. "So you brought a book to read?"

"*Alien Space Lesbians*, you mean? What else would someone bring to read in the woods by moonlight?"

"Were you bringing it to me?"

This was almost definitely flirtatious, and Corinthia paused to think before pressing ahead with full and pure-hearted honesty. "I didn't know you'd be here," Corinthia said. "I just... had a feeling I should go. And I should bring the book. And then there you were, and I accidentally made you fall into a pond."

"I won't let you blame yourself, Corinthia. Where's the fun in that? No, we'll say that I heard you coming, and I fell in on purpose so you could rescue me."

Corinthia laughed and shook her head. "No one would fall into the wetland on purpose."

"I would," Rosemary said, emphatically.

They walked around to the front of the building, where the closest door was the door to the environmental center. Corinthia was not technically supposed to be in the building after closing, either, but she had the key, the code to the security system, and a drenched woman in a silk pajama set.

Another rule, bent like a cracked book spine.

Corinthia paused before the entrance and took off her soaked shoes, setting them neatly aside.

They entered the museum. The lights were off, but the turtle's watery habitat was always lit, as were the aquariums for the fish; and the reptiles had lamps with warm yellow lights at all times. The water pumps burbled away in the background as if someone were putting a pot on to boil.

Corinthia hurried to the little gift shop section and hastily pulled down a souvenir t-shirt—*I Survived Jay Watch 2024*—that looked to be about Rosemary's size. She turned to look back at Rosemary, who was dripping on the rug just inside the entrance, and realized that a t-shirt only solved half the problem of Rosemary's wet clothing.

Corinthia went to the desk where Stevie normally sat and pulled open one of the deeper drawers. Stevie always kept a change of clothes in the drawer—a set of stretchy athletic pants and a pair of no-show socks—for when she wanted to take a run in the Refuge after work. "Thank you, Stevie," Corinthia said briskly, vowing to somehow make up for swiping the stash. "Here," she said to Rosemary. "You can change into these so you won't soak your car on the way home."

Rosemary took the clothes. "You're very kind."

"Yes. Well." Corinthia cleared her throat. "It's the least I can do. You can go and change down the hall, in the bathroom."

"All right, Corinthia," Rosemary said, as if all of it—falling in the pond, the library, the change of clothes—was some sort of delightful game Corinthia had set up for Rosemary's enjoyment. She moved off, no longer dripping quite as much, but still leaving wet footprints on the vinyl floor.

She had almost made it out of the environmental center and into the hallway when she came upon the taxidermied hawk on its wooden perch. Rosemary stopped, shrieked, and flung the clothing into the air. One of the socks landed on the hawk. "What—why would you—why would anyone—*ugh*!" Rosemary turned away from it and shuddered deeply.

Corinthia, baffled by her vehemence but more worried about exposure or shock, quickly gathered the flown clothing, carefully plucking the sock from where it rested like a blindfold over the hawk's glass eyes. "It's just a display."

"It's *dead*," Rosemary countered.

"Sadly. Now put on some dry things before you end up like him." She held the clothes out, with a patented stern look that worked for everything from printers to misbehaving middle schoolers.

Rosemary cocked her head. "Are you *worried* about me?" She didn't wait for an answer. "You *are*," she concluded, with obvious delight. She leaned in and took the clothes, and somehow managed to make it feel like they shared a wonderful, private joke. "How charming!"

Corinthia, who had never been called *charming* in her life, had the feeling that she was rapidly getting in over her head—and the only solution to that, perhaps, was the emergency backup chocolate supply, known as the Coffer of Chocolate, that she kept locked in the breakroom.

8

While Rosemary went off to change, Corinthia went to the breakroom and reached deep into the back of a low cabinet. She pulled out a lightweight but sturdy wooden box, secured with a three-digit combination lock.

It hadn't started as something elaborate. Corinthia had imported a few packets of cocoa here, a few bars of chocolate there, until one day she found that the improvised basket she was using was not only overfull, but terribly, unacceptably unorganized. So she converted a thrifted tea chest and placed everything in blissful order, then pushed it to the back of a cabinet where it would be undisturbed. Her Coffer of Chocolate had soothed her many a time.

She opened it and selected two cocoa packets. These were her own mixture: beautiful red Dutch processed cocoa, Ceylon cinnamon, real cane sugar with a golden color. They could be made with any milk, dairy or otherwise. A worn silver spoon came out, then a few soft picnic napkins with a red-and-white checked pattern. Corinthia turned on the coffee maker and let the plain hot water run into the carafe. She eyed the tiny bottle of brandy still sitting in the box, then took it out and placed it on the counter.

Her feet weren't cold anymore, or if they were, the feeling was faded and academic, like pictures of ice in a discarded book about Alaska.

By the time Rosemary's feet padded along the hallway, two hot cups of cocoa sat steaming and fragrant.

"Hot drinks!" Rosemary cried in delight. Her wet clothes lay over one arm. Though she looked quite normal at first glance, with a longer look the ordinary t-shirt and stretchy pants seemed to have been placed, incongruously, on a classical statue.

"Just some cocoa," Corinthia said. "To warm you up. You seemed to enjoy it so much when you stopped by." To admit that she observed Rosemary's enjoyment made Corinthia a little shy, but she soldiered on.

Rosemary's quick and clever fingers explored the Coffer of Chocolate without hesitation. She unscrewed the bottle of brandy and sniffed. "Oh, my," she said.

"I didn't add that yet," Corinthia reassured her, thinking that perhaps she'd erred, and Rosemary was bothered in some way by alcohol. Corinthia herself did not drink, but she loved the flavor of brandies and liqueurs, and couldn't resist a small, sensible spoonful, for flavoring.

"It's a lovely scent," Rosemary said, patting Corinthia's arm. "Just strong!"

"Would you like to try a drop in your cocoa?"

"Please."

Corinthia spooned a bit into each cup, and gave each another stir to blend. She raised her mug and waited for Rosemary to do the same.

Rosemary lifted her mug with the smallest hesitation, as if this was the first time she'd actually clinked cups with someone, after having only read about it in a book. But what she lacked in initial confidence she made up for with dimples after echoing Corinthia's "Cheers!"

"I hope you're feeling a bit warmer," Corinthia said.

"Much," Rosemary said.

"The brandy doesn't bother you?"

Rosemary shook her head. "My family doesn't"—she paused, seeming to rephrase on the fly—"they don't drink. But I've read good things about it."

"About drinking?"

Rosemary laughed, and Corinthia wanted to inhale it like the aroma of chocolate and fine spirits. "No, librarian Corinthia. About brandy. People in books are always taking it for their health, or to recover from an illness brought on by long walks on the moors."

Corinthia had a sudden image of Rosemary walking the moors, her straight-laced family at home, eating a diet of wholesome nuts, seeds, and spring-water tinctures. "Is your family from around here?"

"Oh, yes. I was born here, as a matter of fact."

Corinthia scoffed. "No one's born in Shadow Ridge. Everyone moves here from somewhere else."

"Not us," Rosemary said, with a look of secret amusement.

Now Corinthia was picturing an entire clan of old-fashioned teetotalers in a creaky Victorian house, neither of which—Victorian houses or teetotalers—likely existed in Shadow Ridge. "You must have gone to school here, then."

"Homeschooled."

Corinthia wanted to ask about college but silenced the too-personal question with a gulp of cocoa instead, which caused her to cough.

"There, there," Rosemary said, thumping her soundly on the back.

"Thank you," Corinthia choked out.

"Here, have some restoring brandy." Rosemary held out the tiny bottle.

Corinthia took it. Unscrewed the cap. Eyed Rosemary like a cozy mystery she wasn't about to give up figuring out, then knocked it back. It burned but gently, right down her throat and into her belly, and all at once she understood what all those historical novels were talking about when they pushed brandy on the cold, weak, and infirm. "Come on," she said, emboldened. "I'll show you my library."

It wasn't Corinthia's library, per se, and she knew that—there were quite a few librarians, clerks, and managers—but a proprietary sense of ownership possessed her and could not be dislodged by mere facts. She led her guest into the library proper.

All the lights were off except for the twinkling white lights strung on the branches of the large artificial tree in the children's section. The glow cast on the floor shifted like moonlight on choppy water, making the bathtubs look even more like small boats adrift in a bay. Any moment, one might float off course and crash into a bookcase cliff.

Rosemary rushed to the nearest boat. It wasn't a run, or a skip, but more of a flutter, and her hands landed on the side of the tub and curled around as she leaned to look inside. "Pillows!" she cried, delightedly.

"They're for reading," Corinthia said, standing a little taller with pride.

"You must climb in them all the time."

"My legs are too long."

"Nonsense," Rosemary said, climbing in. She sank down onto the pillows and leaned back, then threw one leg over the side to dangle as if her toes might actually touch water. "You just stick your leg out."

"I've tried," Corinthia insisted. "It's very awkward."

"You mustn't be afraid to look awkward."

"I'm not afraid."

"Come," Rosemary said, indicating the tub alongside her own. "Sit next to me. I should have helped you in first, but when I saw this tub I had no self-control whatsoever. Will you forgive me? And sit by me?"

Corinthia hid a smile as she added more pillows to the neighboring tub. "I'll sit by you. I want to interrogate you."

Rosemary sat up slightly in mock alarm. "Interrogate me? Whatever for?"

When at last the padding was stable and thick, Corinthia carefully lowered herself into the tub and draped one leg out of it. She rested her arm on the edge of the tub, which brought her close to Rosemary, and at an angle where Rosemary's eyes were shown to startling advantage under the twinkling lights. "Why," Corinthia said, "were you in the Refuge after dark?"

Rosemary relaxed downward and closed her eyes, as if comfortably sinking into the tub. "Why were *you* in the Refuge after dark?"

"I asked you first, in the Refuge, and you never answered me."

Rosemary opened her eyes and looked at Corinthia. "I know why you were in the Refuge."

"Oh, do you?" Corinthia had not missed that Rosemary had dodged the question for the second time, but the lights and the cocoa and possibly the shot of brandy made her willing to let it go, for the moment.

"You were drawn there."

Corinthia felt the truth of this and couldn't deny it. She lay quietly.

"The birds," Rosemary continued. "The sand. The oaks. They called to you. You came."

"They didn't—" Corinthia stopped, because technically they had. "I didn't—" She stopped again when she realized she couldn't answer Rosemary, not fully, because she truly had broken the rules and traipsed through the Refuge at night on the strength of nothing more than a feeling. Instead, she asked, "Is that why you were there? It called to you?"

"No," Rosemary replied, calmly. "It didn't need to. I'm always there."

Homeless, Corinthia thought, with an uncontrollable pang of concern on Rosemary's behalf. But it didn't make sense. No one could camp in the Refuge for long—there was too much foot traffic. Hikers and field trips and bird watchers, not to mention the schoolchildren who wandered around the complex after school, killing time until their parents picked them up. "I didn't mean to startle you."

Rosemary smiled. "I didn't expect you so soon."

"You expected me?"

"When the book disappeared."

"You probably shouldn't store them in a nest," Corinthia said, unable to stifle her inner librarian.

"It wasn't being used anymore," Rosemary pointed out, as if borrowing a bird's nest for storage was a perfectly normal thing to do. "And it's convenient for holding things when I'm walking around."

"I could help you get a library card," Corinthia said, clinging to what still made sense, which was always books.

Rosemary's hand rested on Corinthia's arm, strong fingers and a warm palm. "I know," Rosemary said, and when she said nothing more, they both lay in silence for a minute.

Corinthia tried to understand what had happened—why she had gone back to the Refuge, why Rosemary said such strange things—but under the touch of Rosemary's hand, all those thoughts seemed far away, as if viewed through the wrong end of a telescope, tiny and lacking detail.

"I should go," Rosemary said. She moved her hand away and sat up. "I don't want to get you in trouble."

Corinthia had no fondness for getting in trouble, but when Rosemary stood, Corinthia's heart sank like it had fallen overboard. Corinthia got up and offered her hands to help Rosemary step out of the tub.

Rosemary took Corinthia's hands and alighted. Then, after helping Corinthia in turn, she placed her arm through Corinthia's, and, arm-in-arm like old friends, they walked toward the exterior door. "Do you like the scrub jays?" Rosemary asked.

"Like them? I suppose I like them as well as the next person." Sensing something more was required, and slightly befuddled by Rosemary's closeness, she added, "Actually, I think they're very pretty."

Rosemary's gaze dropped bashfully but her smile grew wide.

They reached the exit, and Corinthia let go so she could open the door for Rosemary.

When Rosemary had exited, she lifted her gaze to meet Corinthia's again, and it was full of mischief. "This is the second time you've shared your chocolate with me."

"Last time you blew me a kiss goodbye," Corinthia said; and this level of daring was quite new to her.

"I could do that again."

"Would you?" Even Corinthia didn't know if her response was doubt or request. The night air couldn't enlighten her, though it rushed through the open door all the same.

When Rosemary chuckled with sweet good humor, Corinthia assumed the declaration had been entirely rhetorical.

Until Rosemary softly cupped Corinthia's face, went on tiptoe, and brushed her lips against Corinthia's.

There were lights sparkling all around, but Corinthia had closed her eyes, and somehow the sparkles became a delicious tingling sensation on her lips; the foundation of the library had disappeared and she was standing on sand; and the roof was gone and starlight fell like soft, cold rain on her skin. The world turned itself inside out and upside down and Corinthia didn't know whether she was falling ill, falling down, or falling in something else entirely.

A breeze whispered across her skin. She opened her eyes.

Rosemary was gone.

The souvenir t-shirt and Stevie's stretchy pants lay in a heap on the ground. Rosemary herself had completely and utterly disappeared.

Corinthia looked left. She looked right. She turned in a circle. She scooped up the clothes and went back inside. She looked in every tub. She peeked down every row of shelves. She glared, finally, at the origami birds over the reference desk, because if they knew anything, they certainly weren't telling.

Corinthia put her hands on her hips.

"And she forgot her book," she said to the empty room.

9

Corinthia attempted to explain the incident over the phone to Stevie the next morning as Beaufort's tail whipped back and forth in anticipation of a walk. She adjusted the phone between her ear and her neck so she could bend down to put on shoes.

"Let me get this straight," Stevie said. "You borrowed my clothes?"

"Yes."

"And then you took her on a tour of the library?" Stevie asked.

"After the cocoa, yes."

"I never knew you hid cocoa at work."

"I have to have some secrets, don't I?"

"Not secrets about chocolate. And especially not about *brandy*. Who are you?"

Corinthia straightened up and leashed the dog. "I'm beginning to wonder." She walked into the kitchen and downed the rapidly cooling dregs of her coffee. There was a strange taste in her mouth—probably what had caused her to have rather odd dreams about eating acorns.

She turned toward the front door when Beaufort pulled in the other direction so hard that Corinthia stumbled. "Beaufort!" she cried. "What's gotten into you?"

Beaufort strained toward the back door.

"Wrong way, dog. We go out the *front* door for walks, remember?" To Stevie, she added, "Sorry, dog's being weird."

Beaufort pulled harder and let out a bay: AWRH-roo AWRH-roo AWRH-roo.

"Must be a bird or a squirrel out there," Stevie said.

"Or a tumbling plastic bag," Corinthia said. "The last time he saw one, he went to Def-Con Five until it was out of sight. I think he thought it was a new kind of raccoon." Corinthia looked out the back window—and froze.

Where once the motley assortment of weeds formed what passed for a lawn, white sand had spilled halfway across the yard, all the way to the base of the wizened grapefruit tree close to the house. Oak tree branches that had previously confined themselves to the Refuge now strained over the top of Corinthia's wooden fence.

The weight of the trees pressed down on the fence so much that it listed at an angle. With any more pressure, it might give up and fall down flat. Between the crush of the trees and the flood of white sand, it looked like the Refuge had risen up and crashed like a breaking wave—but only on Corinthia's yard, and no other.

Beaufort was still pulling and baying, ready to investigate.

"Stevie," Corinthia said, "can you come over?"

"What? Why?"

"Something happened to the backyard."

When Stevie had agreed and Corinthia had directed her to come around the back, they hung up. Corinthia placed the phone carefully on the kitchen counter. She opened the door and walked the dog outside.

In the daily lottery of autumn weather, the sky was blindingly blue and it was already warm outside. Corinthia and Beaufort crossed the small back porch and stepped down into the yard.

There was a clear line where the sand stopped, as if it hadn't been slowly blown in but had been dropped, neatly, like a fluffy white duvet.

Beaufort quieted down and set to pacing back and forth along the edge of the intruding sand, sniffing mightily.

A wind shook the trees. Corinthia even took an involuntary step back, before chastising herself for being silly. She crossed the sand with Beaufort and looked over the sagging fence, where she could now see directly into the Refuge. Dense and tangled trees still obscured the view, but a white sand path wandered into the woods, and invisible birds let out cries of alarm.

What could have done this?

Corinthia walked the dog around the yard until her own footprints chased the dog's paw prints all across the white sand, and tried to understand.

The gate to the side yard banged and Stevie appeared, visibly excited and walking fast—until she caught sight of the sand, the trees, and the listing fence, and stopped in her tracks. "What happened?"

"You tell me, nature expert."

Beaufort was nearly ecstatic with this new turn of events—what could be better than friends *and* a heap of new earth to sniff?—and gamboled happily at the end of the leash.

Stevie greeted the dog with pats. "Tornado?"

"Not a cloud in the sky."

"Earthquake?"

"Neither a shiver nor a quiver. And, you'll notice, the neighbors are untouched."

Stevie surveyed the yards to the left and right, which, like Corinthia's, also bordered the Refuge. "Stampede?"

"Of what? Scrub jays?"

Stevie peered over the fence.

"Also, about last night—I didn't get to tell you..."

Stevie looked at Corinthia. "Tell me what?"

"The end of the story."

Stevie raised her eyebrows.

"She kissed me," Corinthia said.

"She *kissed* you?" Stevie goggled. "And then what, your heart expanded three sizes and knocked the Refuge into your backyard?"

"Don't be ridiculous." Corinthia paused, uncertain whether it was wise to share the next part of the story or not; whether Stevie would think she had taken leave of her senses. "Actually, she kissed me, and then... she disappeared."

"Disappeared? As in ran away?"

"As in *poof*." She related what happened, with less emphasis on the giddy, sparkling magic of the kiss itself. No one had ever made Corinthia feel that way—and therefore, in the bright light of day, it was the least believable part of the whole story.

When she was done, Stevie made a skeptical face. "Corinthia, people don't disappear."

"I know that," Corinthia replied, only slightly defensive. "It was a trick of some kind, of course."

"Of course," Stevie echoed, her gaze drawn back to the Refuge. "And this"—she gestured to the new sand and the lunging trees and the slowly tipping fence—"is clearly some kind of natural phenomenon."

"Clearly," Corinthia said, and they both looked at each other.

Beaufort let out a few more joyful bays in the direction of the Refuge.

"It's like someone he knows is in there," Stevie said. "Who would that be?"

"Probably a hiker who lives in the neighborhood," Corinthia said, wrapping logic around herself like a cozy sweater.

"You don't think it's your lady friend?"

"Are you saying Rosemary is in the woods and Beaufort can sense her, or are you saying she had something to do with this?" Corinthia gestured to the fence.

Stevie shrugged. "*Something's* going on."

"And she's not my 'lady friend.' I don't even know her last name or where she lives."

"You did kiss her."

"*She* kissed *me*. Unexpectedly," Corinthia added, primly.

"Unexpectedly but not un-enjoyably, am I right?"

This was all too much for Corinthia. One didn't meet strangers in the woods and start getting kissed, willy-nilly. Except Corinthia had, and she had too many feelings about it, most of which didn't even seem to have proper names.

If only she could concentrate on something mundane, like shoring up the fence with slats of wood and making calls to her homeowner's insurance company, then everything wouldn't feel so out of control. "Well, I'm glad we cleared this up," she said. She began to walk the dog toward the side yard gate.

"We did?" Stevie said, catching up.

"I'll see you at work after I get Beaufort squared away. I'm sorry I made you rush over," Corinthia added, feeling a bit silly for all the fuss.

"Oh, no problem. How else would I hear stories about you getting naughty in the library and having the Refuge crash your yard?"

"I did not get naughty in the library, thank you very much."

"Don't worry," Stevie said. "It was only a natural phenomenon!"

Corinthia pretended she hadn't heard.

It was a busy morning at work, thanks to the local author festival taking place that day. The library didn't need quiet to be peaceful, and in fact Corinthia welcomed the extra bustle as a pleasant distraction. The plan for the day included a free-flowing meet-and-greet with the authors, followed by lunch for the authors, then a public panel where visitors could ask the authors questions. The day would finish up with a special guided hike for the guest authors, led by Stevie and Corinthia.

Corinthia loved a good plan.

Local writers were allocated tables all around the center of the library. They unfurled their pop-up banners, arranged their stacks of books, and sat behind their tables with expressions of anticipation.

Patrons browsed the tables and wandered into the stacks, and all in all the robust chatter made a nice change to the usual hum of the fluorescent lights.

The Shadow Ridge Library was short on clerks that day, so Corinthia took it upon herself to put some of the returned books back on the shelves. She wheeled one of the small carts into the fiction section and set to work, straightening the already-shelved books as she went and tweaking the angle of the single books that were on display in the empty shelf spaces.

She shelved the rest of the books on the cart, put the cart away, and took a turn around the local author festival. There were thriller, mystery, and romance writers; children's book authors; and a few local history buffs and self-help gurus as well. They sold books, signed them, and chatted with the library patrons who browsed the tables.

To thank the visiting authors and provide them with a midday break, the library ordered in from an Italian restaurant. The breakroom tables were covered with trays of baked ziti, chicken parmigiana, and eggplant parmigiana, plus cheese bread and antipasto salad, and if all that wasn't enough, there were boxes of Italian cookies and cannoli.

Corinthia was sorely tempted by the cannoli. But she refrained, nobly—in the knowledge that if there were some left over, she might partake of one. Or two.

When the authors had finished their lunch, it was time to host the author panel. Corinthia made the announcement over the loudspeaker and headed to the meeting room, where tables and chairs had been arranged ahead of time. The Refuge peeked in the windows, and birds flitted past.

The authors filed in and took their seats behind the table at the front of the room, and the audience shuffled in after. Many of the attendees held notebooks and pens for note-taking.

Corinthia welcomed everyone and introduced each of the authors. Though she used their names to the audience, secretly she had labeled them Mr. Thriller, Ms. Mystery, and Ms. Romance, like characters in a game of Clue but with book genres instead of colors.

Mr. Thriller wrote airport-style books in which a lone man faced down sinister assassins, kidnappers, and government-toppling villains, all of whom could be dispatched in the nick of time with a few well-placed bullets and pithy catch-phrases. His latest was called *Dark Mountain Danger*.

Ms. Mystery wrote cozy sewing-themed mysteries filled with small-town charm, sewing puns, and cat sidekicks. Her most popular book was *Measure Twice, Stab Once*.

Ms. Romance specialized in romance books with witches, vampires, and fairies; occasionally, demons and angels made an appearance. She had broken onto the scene with a steamy paranormal romantic comedy called *Good Witches Make Good Neighbors*.

Corinthia opened the floor to questions and immediately got the old chestnut, "Where do you get your ideas?"

Mr. Thriller jumped in. "My books are ripped straight from the headlines. Just turn on the news and *bam*! There's a story idea." He nodded toward the romance author. "She probably doesn't need any of that. Boy meets girl, yada-yada-yada, there you go."

Ms. Romance looked ready to respond but words tumbled out of Corinthia's mouth before she could think to stop them: "Are you saying romance is simpler than thrillers?"

"It's a formula," Mr. Thriller replied easily.

"And thrillers aren't?"

The audience had perked up, and several people were leaning slightly forward in their chairs.

"Well, maybe," he admitted. "But at least they don't give women unrealistic expectations, am I right?"

"What unrealistic expectations?" Corinthia asked. "Women's happiness? Women's pleasure?"

All heads in the audience swiveled to Mr. Thriller.

"Now we're getting to why women really read those books," he said.

"And why's that?" Ms. Romance asked.

"For the smut!"

The holy zeal in the romance author's eyes could have thrown sparks. "First of all," she said, sitting up straighter, "Not all romances have 'smut.' But if they do, then—like every other tool at the author's disposal—it shows characters not only pursuing pleasure but their own growth as human beings. What do they like? Who are they becoming? Romance novels can reflect all the different ideas of what love can be: sweetness or spice; fluff or thrills; or all of the above! In fact," she continued, "it's not *about* the sex, although there can *be* sex. Romance novels are a safe way to discover what you enjoy in your mind or even in real life. They're a playground for learning about your own happiness."

Mr. Thriller's ears turned slightly pink. "People want realism," he said. "That's not realistic."

"Neither is a man with a mysterious past single-handedly foiling dozens of terrorist plots. If you're allowed to write that over and over again, why can't I write about people finding the best in each other and falling in love?"

The audience seemed to be having a wonderful time, so Corinthia let the conversation play out until she deemed it time to give the poor mystery author a turn. As the questions turned to murder and sewing implements, Corinthia's mind wandered to *Alien Space Lesbians*.

Why *did* the alien fall so desperately in love with the human main character? And why would the human fall in love in return when, as a couple, they were such an obvious mismatch? One from outer space, one from Earth—the cultural conflict alone would be insurmountable.

And yet...

Maybe the human learned to cherish purple scales and unusual eating habits. Maybe the alien was charmed by the human's fanatical love and care of specific furry mammals that were not for eating.

It was not something Corinthia would have understood before, but the author had made it understandable.

A playground for learning about your own happiness.

What would bring Corinthia happiness? Maybe a little sweetness, spice, and fluff, with a dash of thrills like brandy in her cup, for flavor. To share her Cabinet of Chocolate.... to be soothed until she slept in perfect peace.... to be kissed under the twinkling lights of the library tree...

The room had gone silent a beat too long and Corinthia came back to the present with only a slight startle. "I believe that's all the time we have," she said, and wound up the panel with the usual encouragements to buy the authors' books.

Outside, the wind was blowing, and although Corinthia could not feel it on her skin, she felt it in her bones. It was a good thing the guided hike was about to begin, for if she had not been given an excuse to go back to the Refuge, she would have found one and gone anyway.

IO

S tevie had gathered the authors who hadn't been on the panel and was leading them out to the beginning of the shortest and least taxing path, an abbreviated loop that didn't stray too far from the library. Corinthia brought the remaining three authors. All together, they made a large and boisterous group. Corinthia greatly preferred her quiet, solitary walks, but felt it was her duty to help shepherd the visitors around since it had always fallen to Stevie in the past.

Mr. Thriller was already going on about how he was an expert hiker and had managed to work his vast hiking experience into the plot of *Dark Mountain Danger*. It might have been more listenable for Corinthia if she had not already been annoyed by his comments on romance novels.

She dropped back behind the group, hoping the wind and the birds would drown him out. "If there's any justice," she said to herself, "he'll get lost, and the romance author will get the royal treatment from the scrub jays."

It was perhaps not the kindest thought but it was a truthful one, and when Corinthia breathed in the air she felt better than she had before, as if by saying the words she had let them go into the forest, where they could whisper themselves harmlessly into the sand and the trees. When the breeze kicked up, it was as if the forest whispered back.

Corinthia knew it was a fancy and allowed herself to indulge it anyway. She wanted to know the Refuge; she wanted to know Rosemary; and it seemed as if the two were, in some sense, one and the same.

She let the group get even farther away. In the distance a scrub jay stood sentinel on a high branch, watching the clumsy beings traipsing through its home. Corinthia knew herself to be just as heavy-footed as the rest, although she tried to make her footfalls softer.

Rosemary, however, she could not categorize the same way. Rosemary seemed to glide over the sand; to float, almost, as if she weighed nothing and could be carried away on the breeze alone, jeweled headpiece—or buckle, or buttons—catching gems of light and scattering them across the oak leaves like disappearing dew.

I am home, she'd said, and Corinthia could almost believe it.

When the entire group had reached a thicket known for scrub jay activity, Stevie stopped and bid them all to be silent.

It was not quite silent, but shuffled feet and muted voices did not scare away the scrub jays. Their fluttery wingbeats and curious chatter could be heard close by in the tangle of oaks.

"Stay still," Stevie said, loud enough for all to hear but not so loud it would scare the birds.

The romance author from the panel stood still off to one side of the path. A space of white sand lay open next to her.

There was a flash of blue.

A single scrub jay landed in the invitingly open space. It hopped across the sand and paused to peck at the ground.

The authors aimed their cameras and snapped away with murmurs of delight.

Ms. Romance, charmed as would be any object of the scrub jays' attention, simply stood still with a look of wonder on her face.

The scrub jay tilted its head this way and that, and then, upon observing the situation, must have decided it wasn't getting pride of place and so decided to rectify the situation. With another flash of blue and silver, it took off into the air, banked sharply, and landed precisely on the top of the romance author's head.

Her eyes widened with surprise and delight.

"Hold still!" Stevie said, carefully moving into a position to take better photos.

Ms. Romance raised her hands as if to say, *I'm trying!*—and before she could lower them, two more scrub jays shot out of the trees. One landed on each open hand. The romance author at last stood perfectly still, only flinching when the scrub jay on her head decided to give an exploratory *thwack* with its beak. "Ow," she said quietly.

For a moment the woman was a statue, and Corinthia could not help but think of a statue of a saint, covered in birds; how fortunate, how blessed this visitor was to be graced by the scrub jays. How magical.

"I've never seen so many land on a person at once," Stevie said, finally lowering her camera.

As if some signal had been shared between the birds—*They've got enough pictures, let's go!*—all three burst into flight and disappeared into the maze.

Corinthia felt absurdly pleased that her idle wish had been granted, and could not help but allow the unwarranted pride to last all the way back to the covered pavilion where the hike had begun.

Now that the short hike was over, Stevie handed out miniature bottles of water and brochures with more information about the Refuge, including classes, lectures, and the upcoming Wildlife Festival.

"Wait," the romance author said, as they were all about to make their way back to the library. "Where'd that guy go?"

"What guy?" Stevie asked.

"The thriller author from the panel."

It was quickly agreed among the group that Mr. Thriller, as Corinthia had to be careful *not* to call him out loud, had been with the group until approximately the halfway point of the hike. After that, no one could remember seeing him.

Stevie looked uncertain, but also not too concerned. "Maybe he turned back and didn't tell anyone."

"Probably," Corinthia said. Trust Mr. Thriller to lose interest in the Refuge.

The whole party returned to the library. The authors returned to their tables. Corinthia and Stevie lingered by the thriller author's table, which remained, for an increasingly distressing number of minutes, unmanned.

"Maybe he left?" Stevie said.

"And abandoned his seven-foot banner and three dozen copies of his books?" Corinthia replied.

"Maybe he went to the bathroom?"

Corinthia frowned. It was logical. Perhaps Stevie was right. People didn't get lost in the Refuge, anyway. It was bounded on all four sides, like Castle Adventure. Eventually you'd run into a wall, turn around, and find your way out. "Yes," she said. "That must be it."

So Stevie left for the environmental museum, and Corinthia returned to the circulation desk until it was almost closing time and everyone was packing up to go. The authors filed out, hauling their carts and tote bags, until at last the library was as it had been before.

Except for Mr. Thriller's table. The banner and books were untouched, and there was no sign of their owner.

Corinthia returned to the desk and picked up the phone. "Stevie," she said, "his stuff is still here."

"Did you see him come back?"

"No."

"Maybe we should check the parking lot."

It was a good idea, Corinthia thought. The authors and patrons would be gone. "Meet me outside," she said, and when Stevie agreed, Corinthia hung up. As part of the closing procedure, she checked the bathrooms, which were empty.

She passed through the revolving door and her sense of unease increased.

The last remaining vehicle had a bumper sticker that said *Warning: Author with an Attitude.*

"That's our guy," Corinthia said to Stevie.

Stevie looked at Corinthia. "You don't think he's still... in there?"

"In the Refuge? Surely not." She paused. "Maybe."

"Should we call the police?"

"Why? The Refuge is open until the sun sets; he's an experienced hiker; and there's no reason he would be in danger." Corinthia felt momentarily guilty for wishing he'd get lost, and reconsidered. "Maybe we should look for him."

"If he's in there, he could be anywhere," Stevie said.

There were dozens of paths, some no more than rabbit trails, all of which criss-crossed and doubled back. Corinthia imagined that if only Beaufort were there, she would give him one of Mr. Thriller's books to sniff, and off the dog would go, in hot pursuit, his characteristic bay echoing over through the trees, setting the scrub jays to flight. Of course Beaufort had never done any such thing, but it was certainly an amusing thought.

"We could at least walk the main trails and call his name," Corinthia said. She imagined shouting *Mr. Thriller*, and had to stifle a laugh that seemed to come from nerves rather than humor.

"Okay," Stevie agreed. "Let's leave a note on his car and his author table, in case he comes back, though. With my phone number."

They did so, and returned to the entrance to the Refuge. It was the only way out—all paths branched from this one, eventually; and even someone who *wasn't* an expert hiker could have used the location of the sun to head in the direction of the library generally.

They hiked the main trail. They called Mr. Thriller's real name. They looped onto the secondary trail and did the same.

The sun slowly sank toward the western horizon.

"He could have gone around us and gone back to his car," Stevie said.

Corinthia nodded. All the way back to the library, the scrub jays were talking, as if something exciting was happening.

The writer-with-an-attitude car? Still parked.

The author table? Still decorated.

Missed calls? None.

"Now we call the police?" Stevie said, as they thumbed through copies of *Dark Mountain Danger*.

Mr. Thriller could actually write, Corinthia mused as she skimmed the pages. It was always irritating when someone who personally annoyed her turned out to be good at something. "Let's look one more time," she said. "If he were in trouble, wouldn't he have used his phone to call for help?"

"Maybe it ran out of battery."

Corinthia had nothing to say to that, but her stomach sank like the sun, and she didn't know why.

When they returned to the Refuge, the sky had turned a most aggressive shade of pink, as if it were determined to be noticed despite Corinthia's distress.

In fact, everything around her practically glowed with beauty and a show-off sense of self-satisfaction: *See how soft the sand? How sweet the evening breeze? How delightful the distant wingbeats keeping time?*

All of it, all of it, all was for her, and Corinthia not only did not understand but felt actively frightened.

Mr. Thriller was lost in the Refuge. This, she believed.

And she suspected it was all her fault.

II

They were back in the Refuge before Corinthia plucked up her courage to say something. "It's my fault, Stevie."

"What's your fault?"

"The author getting lost. I did it."

Stevie scoffed. "Don't be ridiculous. How did *you* make a man get lost in the woods?"

"I wished for it, Stevie! I stood there in the Refuge at the beginning of the hike and I wished the romance author would meet scrub jays and I wished he would *literally* get lost and it happened!"

"Slow down, there, my friend. You made a wish? What, like with a birthday cake?"

"I was angry about what he said at the panel and I dropped back where no one could hear me and I said it. I said I hoped he would get lost. Everything I said came true!"

Stevie shook her head. "Coincidence."

"Why did the birds swarm that woman like she was covered in birdseed?"

"They didn't exactly swarm—"

"You've seen three of them land on someone like that, then?"

"Well, no—"

"*I summoned birds.*"

"Corinthia, you're scaring me—"

"*You're* scared? *I'm* scared! What is this? What is happening to me?"

"Nothing is happening to you! It's just a coincidence, that's all."

Stevie said further comforting words but Corinthia was only half-listening. When Stevie stopped, Corinthia continued. "He wasn't even a bad guy, just a few stupid opinions! Now he's gone and we can't find him and I didn't mean to and—"

"Corinthia, you didn't do anything!"

Their steps had been quick-time on the path, in rhythm with their words, but at this Corinthia stopped. She closed her eyes, felt her weight supported by the sand beneath her feet. "I didn't mean to, Stevie, I swear, I was only being petty and silly and impulsive and I'm *never* that way and I *never* thought the forest was listening to every word I said, it's my fault, it's all my fault…"

There was a rasping, unscrewing sound, and then Corinthia was hit in the face with the contents of a full mini-bottle of water. "Snap out of it!"

Corinthia sputtered. "What—" She wiped her face with her sleeve. "Why did you do that?"

"Because you were clearly losing hold of your faculties."

Corinthia continued to dab at her face and brush at her clothes. The cold water, unwelcome and shocking as it may have been, brought back clarity. "I was, wasn't I."

"Talking about some guy getting lost was all your fault," Stevie chided.

"No," Corinthia said, thoughtfully. "That part was right."

"Don't make me get another water bottle."

"Stevie," Corinthia said, placing her hands on her smaller friend's shoulders and looking into her worried face. "I haven't lost my faculties. I'm telling you something's changed. I've changed. Something is different."

"Oh…kay," Stevie said, clearly not convinced.

"Please don't be frightened."

"I'm not frightened," Stevie said. "I just don't understand."

Corinthia let go of Stevie's shoulders. Wind dried her face as thoroughly as a mother with a soft towel. Her understanding of the world was unfolding and refolding, like an origami bird deconstructed and rebuilt into something new. The grains of sand beneath her feet were diamonds; the trees, molten silver. All at once all of the birds knew her and she knew all the birds, could have pointed them out one by one no matter where they hid. Same for the tortoises and snakes and the spiders—my God, there were so many spiders!—and among all this small life it was easy, now, to sense one man wandering in the distance. "I found him," Corinthia said, simply.

"You found him," Stevie repeated, her words full of doubt.

"I can sense him. I can sense... everything."

"You sure you don't want to sit down? There's a bench up ahead—"

"It's okay," Corinthia said. "I'm okay."

Stevie looked at her friend with concern. "All right, then," she said, slowly. "You say you found him?" She gestured to the trail, as if to say, *Prove it*.

The sunset light made everything pink and surreal. Corinthia moved through the maze like she'd built it herself, movable walls and all. The birds cheered her on. Stevie hurried to keep up.

Past the Ephemeral Wetland. Off the main trail to a branch angling south-southwest. Sneakers squeaking on clean white sand touched with sparkles, trees shivering in the wind as it changed direction.

How wonderful it felt, how *right*, to finally know what to do and be able to do it. They walked and walked until at last they turned a corner—

And there was Mr. Thriller, crouching to examine a blueberry bush.

"Where were you?" cried Stevie.

The author stood up and dusted his hands. "I don't know how I got here," he said, "but I think I got turned around a bit."

"You think?" Stevie said.

"I was with the group, and then I walked off on a side trail—thought it might add some flavor to the scene I was working on—and then I looked around and everyone was gone. So I've been circling around, I guess, trying to find my way out."

"What about your phone?" Corinthia said. "Why didn't you call someone?"

Mr. Thriller put his hands on his hips and looked down at the ground, briefly, before meeting her gaze again. "After telling everyone I was a great hiker? Ha! A right fool I'd look, calling for help from a little old nature preserve. No, I figured I'd wander out eventually."

Not if the little old nature preserve didn't let you go, Corinthia thought. But a small gray cloud of lingering guilt made her bring him out of himself as the three of them walked back. She asked him questions about his next book—authors loved that sort of thing—and kept him talking about *High Mountain Hazard* until they had him safely back in the parking lot, loaded up with his books and his banner, seemingly none the worse for wear.

He apologized for being a bit "salty," as he put it, about romance novels, and confessed to a recent tough time of personal problems that he was working to overcome. He asked Corinthia and Stevie for romance novel recommendations, and Corinthia pressed cash on him for a copy of *Dark Mountain Danger*, which he signed *To Corinthia: Thanks for the hike!*

Corinthia laughed weakly.

He got in his car. The palm trees outside the library carved shadows from the dim yellow streetlights, and the tips of the palm fronds wiggled in the breeze, looking like nothing so much as someone showing off freshly polished fingernails.

They waved until he drove out of sight.

"Are you sure you didn't pick up any of those crystals?" Stevie said.

"No crystals."

"You want to explain what's going on?"

"I want to figure out what's going on." Corinthia had only the fact of what she had experienced, and no explanation for it whatsoever. "I'm fine," she said. "Everything is fine."

"Is it, though?"

"It is," Corinthia said, severely. "And tomorrow I shall fix my fence."

"You shouldn't be fixing a sandwich, let alone a fence."

"*Drew* shall fix my fence," Corinthia amended.

Stevie perked up. "Does she need help?"

"Probably not—"

"Snacks! I'll bring... homemade cupcakes!"

"Stevie, you can't cook to save your life."

"Store-bought cupcakes!"

"Handywomen," Corinthia said, "don't need cupcakes."

"No," Stevie said, waggling her eyebrows, "but I need a handywoman."

"Is that all you can think about? Your love life?"

"What else is there?" Stevie cried, spinning around and throwing her arms in the air.

Corinthia considered. Up until a few days previous, she would have thought that the most satisfying life required only air-conditioning, books, dogs, chocolate, and friendship.

But strange things were happening, and now nothing was quite the same.

12

Even before Corinthia saw the contents of the bed of Drew's truck, she could smell the cut wood, the gasoline in a bright red plastic canister, and the lingering smell of exhaust around the chainsaw. "You came prepared," Corinthia said.

"Yup," Drew said, dropping the tailgate with a controlled *bang*.

Stevie's eyes widened.

"Would you like some help carrying all that?" Corinthia asked, secretly hoping the answer would be "No."

Drew raised one eyebrow and smirked. "You two, with your soft hands? Nah, I got this."

Stevie held her hands out. "Mine aren't *too* soft, are they?"

Drew looked them over with a professional eye, and then not-so-professionally took one of Stevie's hands and gave it a long, slow, up-close look. "They're just right," she said.

Stevie giggled.

Corinthia rolled her eyes. "Maybe we should get out of the way and let Drew get to work."

"That's what you're paying me for," Drew agreed cheerfully, and began hauling pieces of lumber out of the truck.

Stevie elbowed Corinthia solidly in the ribs when Drew had walked off bearing half a tree's worth of wood. "I was *getting* somewhere."

"Yes, but my fence wasn't."

"Spoilsport."

"Coquette."

"Who even *uses* words like that?"

"I do," Corinthia said, a lifetime's use of five-dollar words giving her a blithe serenity about it. "Besides, you can get back to it when you serve the refreshments."

They retreated to the kitchen, where Beaufort had taken up a post by the back door to watch the goings-on. His gaze followed Drew back and forth almost as much as Stevie's did, only Stevie didn't occasionally let out an observant howl or two to mark the occasion.

Corinthia had done the research and determined that to get her homeowner's insurance company involved would be more trouble than it was worth. They might replace the broken fence—but they might also cancel the policy at the end of year, as a lesson to all homeowners who might dare to make a claim on the insurance they paid thousands of dollars for.

So Corinthia hired Drew to prop it up, safely—until the day, presumably far in the future, when Corinthia had enough cash to pay for a full repair or replacement.

Stevie fussed with the snacks: opening and closing the cupcake box, checking Corinthia's supply of ice, rearranging bottles of water and soda, popping open the bag of chips, tucking the wrapped sub sandwich sections into a real basket lined with red-checked cloth.

"I'll have to fix my fence more often," Corinthia said, "if you're going to lay out a spread like this."

Beaufort, temporarily distracted by the scent of Genoa salami, tavern ham, and capicola, turned his head, but then resumed his close observation of the new stranger in the backyard.

"I'm just being nice," Stevie said.

"You're seducing her with submarine sandwiches."

"Is that illegal?"

"It could be considered false advertising, since you don't cook."

"*She* cooks."

"So you're only flirting with her for her domestic labor."

"Is that what they're calling it these days?" Stevie's appreciative gaze went to where Drew was hefting and moving and looking altogether quite strong and capable. "Speaking of true love, have you seen Rosemary again?"

"Why is that 'speaking of true love'?"

Stevie tore her gaze away from Drew to give Corinthia a look. "Because you get a sort of stupid look whenever you talk about her."

"I do not."

"Also because she *kissed* you." Stevie shook her head. "You've gone so long without stars in your eyes, Corinthia, that you don't even recognize them when they twinkle."

Corinthia opened her mouth to retort, then shut it. Dry spells didn't scare or shame her, but *missing* something? It couldn't be borne. "I would recognize twinkling," she finally said.

"Hmm," Stevie replied, noncommittally.

"I would," Corinthia insisted.

"Of course you would."

"Just because I don't giggle and make goo-goo eyes doesn't mean I can't be romantic."

"You'd be terrible at making goo-goo eyes and giggling. All you need to do is be yourself and stick to your strengths."

Corinthia wondered what her strengths might be. Good taste in books, for one. Excellent organizational skills. Tidiness. Cocoa-making ability. All very nice but probably not what people thought of first when seeking romance, except for maybe the cocoa part, which Rosemary seemed to like quite a lot.

"You want people to think you're all stuffy," Stevie continued, "but in reality, you care a lot."

"I do?"

"You care about your dog. You care about me. You care about our dinky old street, for heaven's sake. You care about people finding the books they're looking for in the library. You even care about the Refuge, now. You're civic and you're thoughtful and it's going to be catnip for a certain type of person."

"What type of person?"

"Someone who brings you out of yourself a bit. Makes you step out of your comfort zone but holds your hand at the same time."

Corinthia folded her hands one over the other, self-consciously, as if someone might leap out and try to grab one.

She looked out the window, where Drew was manhandling, or woman-handling, a large piece of lumber into place. "I bet she could use an extra pair of hands," Corinthia said, nodding toward the backyard.

Stevie didn't look back as she opened the back door, jumped lightly down the step, crossed the small porch, and hurried across the patchy lawn until it became white sand.

Beaufort, startled by this development, let out a few more tuneful howls.

"Hush, dog," Corinthia said, smoothing the hound's ears and patting his back. "Let them talk."

Drew was already slipping work gloves onto Stevie's hands. Both women were laughing. Corinthia smiled and helped herself to a chilled soda.

When Stevie and Drew burst in, later, flushed of cheek and sweaty of brow, they brought the oak and sand scent with them.

"All done?" Corinthia asked.

"Almost," Drew said, tossing her ball cap aside.

Beaufort leaped for it, but luckily it had landed on the kitchen counter, out of reach.

"I told Drew she deserved a break after working so hard," Stevie said.

Drew noticed the array of food and drink. "You did all this for me?"

"It was Stevie's idea," Corinthia said. "She thought since you cook for a living, you should have a break."

Drew hooked an arm around Stevie's shoulders and gave her an affectionate hair ruffle.

Stevie fairly glowed. As soon as Drew was looking the other way, Stevie gave Corinthia a covert thumbs-up.

Drew pulled out a chair and began helping herself to a wrapped section of the sub. "You ever get to read that book?" she asked Corinthia.

"I started it."

"What'd you think?"

Corinthia considered. She liked to wait until she was finished with a book to evaluate it, but she did have a few thoughts formed. "Is that how it would really happen if an alien space lesbian landed on Earth? Would she fall in love with the first human woman she ran into?"

"That's, like, fate," Drew said. She washed down another bite with cola straight from the can.

"It could happen," Stevie chimed in.

"And why would the human agree to fly off into space, anyway? I feel like that's dangerous."

"You would," Stevie scoffed.

"Nah," Drew said. "Think about it. She may be purple and scaly but she's beautiful, she's competent, and she's clearly rich enough to own a spaceship. I'd board that," she added, matter-of-factly.

"Me too," Stevie said.

"You're a romantic," Corinthia said to Stevie. "Your opinion doesn't count. At least Drew has some logic behind hers."

"You think you're logical," Stevie said, "but wait till a purple alien lands on your lawn."

"Good luck to her picking the sandspurs out of her webbed, purple alien feet."

"Huh," Drew said, thoughtfully. "I wonder if real aliens are purple."

Stevie and Corinthia traded a look.

"What do you mean, 'real' aliens?" Stevie said.

"You know," Drew said, waving half a sub around. "Like the TV show, *The X Files*?"

Corinthia had a habit of scowling at things she found far-fetched, but she tried very hard not to make a face. A warning glance from Stevie told her she hadn't quite succeeded.

"Have you ever looked at one of those pictures from the James Webb Space Telescope?" Drew said.

Corinthia and Stevie looked at each other, eyebrows raised, before both of them shook their heads.

Drew pulled out her phone, tapped a few times, and displayed a photo that appeared to contain a field of bright, multicolored lights against inky black space. "Looks like stars, right?" She paused, heightening the mystery. "Each one of those is a galaxy. A *galaxy*. Galaxies contain more than a hundred billion stars each. So, just in this section of space: thousands of galaxies. Billions and billions of stars."

"The mind boggles," Stevie said.

"Boggles is right," Drew replied. "Why couldn't there be something special out there?"

"Or here," Corinthia murmured, before realizing she'd spoken aloud.

"Pardon?" Stevie said.

"Nothing."

"I think there could be aliens," Stevie said, in her most *I'm-open-minded* voice. Stevie was indeed very open-minded to crystals, but not so much to things that required biological proof. She cracked open the cupcake box in an attempt—transparent to Corinthia—to change the subject. "Would you like a cupcake?"

Drew thanked her and added the dessert to her plate, then continued with the topic. "There's a million planets out there, right? So even million-to-one odds are good."

"Still better odds than finding a date here on planet Earth," Stevie said. Then her gaze went to Drew, who apparently ate cupcakes by licking off the icing first. Stevie cleared her throat. "Although sometimes we get lucky."

Drew met Stevie's gaze with a smile. The smidge of frosting that had ended up on her cheek like a beauty mark made it an even better smile. "Sometimes."

Corinthia didn't know how they made it look so easy. Sure, Stevie had needed a little push to get going, but once she was going... look at her! Bantering, laughing; no doubt they would have each other's phone numbers by the time Drew got back in her truck.

Corinthia, on the other hand, felt as bewildered as she had the first time she walked the Refuge. She wasn't effortlessly funny, or vivacious, or capable of slinging double entendres around like a handywoman with a pile of two-by-fours.

"So, what happened to your fence, anyway?" Drew asked. "Storm blow it down?"

"Yes," Stevie said, at the same time as Corinthia said, "No."

They looked at each other.

"No," Stevie said, at the same time as Corinthia said, "Yes."

Drew propped her chin on her hand and looked from Corinthia, to Stevie, and back again.

"You believe in aliens, right?" Corinthia said.

Drew nodded.

"How about unexplained phenomena?"

Drew leaned back in her chair and crossed her arms. "Try me."

Despite Corinthia's many rules of self-conduct, she was not a mistrustful person. Thoughtful, yes. Prone to judgment, certainly. But she judged Drew to be unlikely to be ruffled by the story, and so she shared the details of the strange occurrences that had taken place in and around the Refuge: the lost and found book, the mysterious appearance and disappearance of Rosemary, the forest versus the fence, and the lost and found author.

"Whoa," said Drew. "That's...

"Weird?" said Corinthia.

"Awesome," Drew finished. "And this Rosemary chick," she added, "what's she got to do with it?"

Corinthia did not necessarily approve of calling women "chicks," but decided to allow it on the grounds that Drew was clearly well-intentioned, if a bit prone to casualness. Also, Stevie would probably *like* being called a chick. "*Do* with it?" Corinthia echoed. "Nothing, I suppose."

"I mean, she always seems to be *around*, right?"

"She hasn't been around my fence."

"You know what she means," Stevie said.

Corinthia felt suddenly protective of Rosemary. If she had been standing in the room, Corinthia might even have considered putting an arm around her. "Rosemary," she said, "did not vandalize my fence."

"Not *vandalize*," Stevie said. "But maybe she knows something. Because she's in the Refuge so much."

"You should go back in there," Drew said, pointing at Corinthia with what was left of the cupcake.

Stevie lit up. "You should do the forest bathing activity tomorrow!"

"I should do what exactly?" Corinthia said.

"We should all go!" Stevie was bouncing up and down, now, making a face at Corinthia that was clearly intended to strongarm her into playing wingwoman.

"Is it, like, swimming or something?" Drew asked. She seemed to be open to the idea even if it did involve being immersed in actual water.

"There's no bathing involved," Stevie said. "You just stand around in the woods and… commune with the forest. The guy who runs it is super nice and we get like twenty people showing up every time we offer this program."

"I'm in," Drew said, nonchalantly, as if forest bathing was something she did every day and twice on Sunday.

"Yippee!" cried Stevie. "Corinthia?"

Corinthia had never been a granola type of person, this was true. But in a part of herself Corinthia had heretofore not acknowledged, an unruliness had awoken—and secretly thrilled to the invitation.

"I'll go," she said.

13

S tanding at the edge of the Refuge the following day, Corinthia had second thoughts. Her previous forays had been blessed with cool air; changeable, cloud-skirted skies; and a breeze that ran down the paths like a child at a birthday party. But today, it was hot.

"Hot" in the Refuge didn't mean the same thing as "hot" anywhere else. The sun poured from an endless blue sky, bounced off the white sand, and baked any exposed skin without mercy. Shorts had seemed like a good idea until Corinthia's calves began to crisp.

"Stop fussing," Stevie said, when Corinthia pointed this out. "Drew's not complaining."

Drew had wandered off a little ways and was drinking from a tan-colored canteen.

"Drew," Corinthia pointed out, "appears to be wearing lightweight technical gear suitable for a two-week jungle trek."

"You'll be fine," Stevie said. "We'll move further in and there'll be more shade."

The event leader waved his arms. "Come along, everyone. We're going to go a little ways down the trail." He looked more like a fisherman than the crunchy granola type Corinthia had been expecting. His broad-brimmed hat cast shade on his weathered face, and his khaki shirt and pants had what looked like a very practical quantity of pockets. Corinthia respected dressing for the occasion.

A single black vulture, feathers shining in the sun, glided elegantly overhead like a black satin kite. Corinthia had seen birds of its kind while walking Beaufort. On the ground they seemed to be ungainly, but over the Refuge they seemed to be a special sort of observer, content to float between the sand and sky.

In the intense light, the dragonflies looked like suncatchers carved from brown gemstones.

When their group had gathered in the relative coolness of one of the trail corridors walled by thickets, he waved to everyone. "I'm George, and I am a certified forest bathing guide. Has anyone here been forest bathing before?"

Stevie's hand shot up.

"Good, good. Well, if you've never forest bathed before, don't worry. It's as easy as falling off a log!" He gestured to a nearby fallen tree, and chuckled. "We're just going to open up our senses and find some tenderness for the forest."

"Tenderness?" Corinthia muttered.

Stevie elbowed her.

"Remember," he said. "This is not a hike. Take your time. Slow down. It's okay to stay in one spot for the whole session! You have everything you need right here." He gestured to the immediate vicinity with one hand, but he also touched the center of his chest with the other. "Use all five of your senses, not just your eyes and ears. Smell the dirt. Touch the trees. Taste the pine needles."

"Taste the what now?" Corinthia said.

"They're edible," Stevie said.

"First, however," he continued, "I always like to start with one of my favorite opening activities: asking a question of the forest."

Corinthia would previously have thought this was ridiculous, but since she had basically already bossed the forest around with accidental wishes, she figured she could handle asking it a simple question.

"I want everyone to find a tree that you feel drawn to—or even a flower, you can speak into it like a telephone—and ask it a question. Out loud, mind you: like you mean it. And then when we get done, we'll see if we got any answers."

Drew nodded as if this was all as believable as aliens.

"I am not," Corinthia said, quietly, "speaking into a flower like a telephone." Communicating with the forest was one thing. Looking silly was quite another.

"Oh, yes, you are," Stevie said.

Drew was already peering into a thicket, looking for a likely conversationalist.

"Go talk to a tree," Stevie commanded, and then scampered off after Drew.

Corinthia shook her head, but the motion seemed to catch the attention of the guide, who wandered over.

"Having trouble finding a tree to talk to?" he said, as if this was the most normal thing in the world to discuss.

"I guess so," admitted Corinthia. It was just the right amount of truth to spare his feelings: she did not want to find a tree, and therefore was having trouble finding a tree.

He stood, unfazed and rooted, simply nodding and looking at her with calm kindness. "Why don't we try body radar?"

Corinthia did not like the sound of body radar. "What's that?"

"You just close your eyes," he said, matching movement to words, "and you hold your hands out, and you *feel*"—there was that word again—"until you notice something."

"'Notice' something?"

He opened his eyes, as if this was all the explanation needed.

"Notice something," she repeated.

"*Feel* something," he amended.

"So should I be noticing something or feeling something?"

He gently patted her shoulder. "Why not both?" And with that, he ambled away to where a small group of people were on hands and knees, speaking into tiny buds on wild blueberry shrubs.

Stevie and Drew were nowhere to be seen.

Corinthia sighed. Why did it have to be woo-woo? Why couldn't it just be matter of fact? When she found Mr. Thriller, it was all *right there*, no fuss.

She could do this. And she could do it her way.

She closed her eyes. She held out her hands, tentatively, not quite extending them all the way, vaguely hoping that no one was actually looking at her. *There's nothing to it*, she thought.

*It was there before, it will be there again, even if it seems like
there's nothing to feel except this flaming-hot heat—*

And there it was.

Soft, at first, like the lights of the library tree seen at a distance through half-closed eyes: little pinpoints of silver.

Corinthia's eyes flew open. The sun dazzled the silver specks into nonexistence. Hesitantly, reluctantly, she closed her eyes again, this time stretching her arms out all the way, hands open, palms out.

Twinkle, twinkle, little stars—there they were again.

For the first time in a very long time, Corinthia remembered what it was like to play outside as a child: the tyranny of time, fallen away; the contentment of roaming a place that belonged to you whether you owned it or not; freedom, golden and fleeting as the rays of the setting sun.

This time, when she opened her eyes, she did so slowly, carefully, taking care to notice where the specks had been.

A pine tree. They had been around a plain old pine tree, not too tall, with bunches of needles so fresh and green that, in the wind, they looked like exuberantly shaken pom-poms.

"I guess it's you, then," Corinthia said. She moved over to the tree, casually, hoping no one would take notice, or, heaven forbid, follow. She gently took hold of a low branch and pulled one of the pom-poms closer; after all, if a thing was worth doing, it was worth doing right. "Could you"—she paused, considering—"could you please explain to me why all these weird things are happening?"

The sky could have opened, or trumpets sounded, or any number of strange and wonderful things, but there was only the distant call of an eastern towhee. *Kweep!*

"Excellent," Corinthia said, letting go of the branch and brushing off her hands quickly. "That was extremely helpful." She had used body radar as instructed, found a tree, and asked it a question. Duty fulfilled. She returned to where the guide was already beginning to explain the next activity.

"I promise we'll spend the rest of the time just soaking it all in," he said, "but I want you to try this one activity because I always feel like we have a lot of fun with it."

When the guide had finished explaining, Corinthia had to admit it did sound kind of fun. They were to choose a section of the trail and define it as a room; give it a name; notice details like the furniture, or decor, or where the windows and doors might be; and take note of the quality of light and the aroma.

Just like a home, he said. Or a "green mansion."

Corinthia, who had already drawn a parallel to Castle Adventure during her past trips, was both pleased by her own initiative and a bit embarrassed to have already been playing such a game without even being told to do so.

"Let's go this way," Stevie said. "I know the perfect place."

Corinthia and Drew followed.

The trail turned sharply like a hallway corner before opening into a space, about twice the size of Corinthia's living room, that was defined by a carpet of brown pine needles. The surrounding trees were less dense than in the hallway; less tangled; and Corinthia could see individual oak tree trunks, low-lying palmettos, and several more types of bushes she couldn't identify. Beyond the pine needle carpet lay a small, sparkling body of water, and she realized that this was the smaller of the two Ephemeral Wetlands, only approached from a different angle.

"Ta-da!" said Stevie.

"Cool," Drew said, appreciatively crossing her arms and giving Stevie an approving nod.

"I think this is a living room," Stevie said. "The pine needles make up the shag carpet. And this palmetto cluster—if you squint, it's one of those oversized couches. The small bushes are ottomans. And if you look through the trees this way"—she pointed to the trunks framing the view of the water—"those are windows looking out on the lawn. It needs to be cut," she added, pointing to the grass that poked out of the edge of the wetland. "The branch on the ground is one of those driftwood coffee tables with a glass top—invisible, see?—and you could sit here in the afternoon and look out on the neighborhood and drink your coffee, or your hot chocolate, or what have you."

"All right," Drew said, clearly impressed and ready to build on Stevie's riff. "Check this out," Drew gestured to what, at first, seemed like nothing more than a wall of branches. "It's a food truck."

Stevie and Corinthia came over and gave the area a closer look.

The low, round bushes made convincing wheels. The shape of the trees suggested the body of the vehicle, and the break in the foliage created a pass-through. Corinthia could imagine hot dogs and frothy orange drinks being handed out. Playing "green mansions" was like cloud-watching, only the visions didn't dissolve with the wind. Corinthia knew she would see this "food truck" from that day forward, unfailingly, whenever she passed by this area of the Refuge.

"What about you, Corinthia?" Stevie said.

Corinthia turned and looked down a path. It was one she had been down before, but now she saw it differently. "I see library shelves," she said, "made of branches. And leaf-colored books in a row."

The guide approached. "Did you all find any green mansions?"

"A living room, a food truck, and a library," Stevie reported.

He reached for a nearby branch. "You could serve this on your food truck." It was one of the same kind of pine tree Corinthia had conversed with. He pulled off a few of the newest, greenest needles, and handed them to Corinthia, Stevie, and Drew. Then he popped one in his own mouth and chewed. "Not bad. Makes a nice tea. Mighty interesting soda, too."

Drew bit into her pine needle first. She chewed thoughtfully. "Citrusy," she said.

"Good, huh?" Stevie said, nibbling her own needle.

Had Corinthia been alone in the Refuge, there might not have been enough motivation to put a piece of a tree in her mouth—but with Stevie, Drew, and the genial guide happily chowing down, she felt it would be unreasonable not to join them.

She bit down on the pine needle, fearful it would have a jagged edge against her tongue, but it was not too rough, and it released its flavor not unlike a thin shred of fresh sugar cane between her teeth. Meyer lemon candy, she thought instantly. Just like the ten-cent wrapped candy sticks from when she was a child.

The forest guide regarded her with a benignly curious expression. "Did you get an answer to your question?"

"Not yet," Corinthia said.

He nodded thoughtfully. "Have you tried giving something back to the forest?"

"Not recently."

"You might try that." He ambled off again, this time to a group who appeared to have laid full-out on the sand to enthusiastically point out shapes in the clouds.

"I think that's a lovely idea, to give back to the forest," Stevie said. "What shall we give?"

Drew was already pouring a little water on a thirsty-looking patch of moss. "Want to pour some water?" Drew asked Stevie.

"Oh, yes please!"

While they were occupied sprinkling the plants with the remaining water in the canteen, Corinthia quietly sidled down one of the trails. She stopped in front of a tree she recognized as a silk bay, one with smooth and fragrant leaves. She looked up and down the trail to make sure no one was watching.

Then she silently kissed two fingertips, and pressed them
against one perfect leaf.

149

14

ROSEMARY'S INTERLUDE

Rosemary stood on the crest of the tallest ridge in the Refuge and looked down over the green maze. She didn't need a staff to keep her footing, but she had picked up a gnarled oak branch in a fit of nervousness, and was rolling it lightly between her palms.

A worry stick, she thought to herself. Larger than a worry stone, for larger worries.

The sun had fallen below the horizon, and all the visitors to the Refuge had left. Rosemary was alone; or, at least, she appeared to be.

The white sand swirled around her feet as if in a sudden breeze.

Rosemary glanced at the dancing sand. "You can't get carried away," she said. "You'll scare her. You're too much."

The sand fizzed upward rebelliously before it settled in a grumbly pattern.

Rosemary sighed. After meeting Beaufort, she could no longer think of the forest as anything but an over-enthusiastic dog, one who tended to jump up on unsuspecting visitors and knock them over.

The trees were talking, too, now; making plans, no doubt, of what to do next. Rosemary could hear them whispering among themselves.

"I said *no*," Rosemary added firmly.

A few nearby scrub jays attempted to scold the trees into line. Rosemary appreciated the solidarity but didn't rely on it counting for much. The forest did what it wanted. And the forest, like Rosemary herself, had become fascinated by the Shadow Ridge librarian.

Rosemary couldn't blame the forest—a few encounters with Corinthia, and she, too, found herself with entirely un-reasonable feelings.

Perhaps it had been forward to return Corinthia's wallet to her home when she could have reasonably dropped it off at the library's circulation desk the next day.

It also might not have been entirely reasonable to fall into the pond so that Corinthia could rescue her.

But, oh, the delicious chocolate. The snug little cottage stuffed with books. The silly hound. The starlit library. The kiss! There were so many books to discuss, so many secrets to share with the dignified, intelligent, fascinating librarian... ah, Corinthia!

Rosemary could not help a blissful sigh.

As if conjured, a breeze arrived and rolled over the green maze like a great hand ruffling the branches.

Her whole life she had remained hidden. Watching. Waiting. Learning. Taking only the most careful forays out of the Refuge, until one day she entered the Shadow Ridge Library and met a librarian, and every caution was thrown to the wind. No wonder the forest had become involved—it was quite literally the most natural thing.

Rosemary plucked a leaf from a nearby branch. "We will take it slowly," she said, hoping the forest would listen. She rubbed the leaf with her fingers and inhaled the faint scent—a discarded plant identification book had described silk bay leaves as having an aroma reminiscent of soap and licorice. Soap she had found in the library restrooms, but licorice was as faraway a concept as the moon.

Despite working up the courage to actually enter the Shadow Ridge Library—rather than just quietly raid the free book cart—Rosemary felt increasingly unsure that her haphazard education would be sufficient to mix in society.

I will learn, she reminded herself. *Even if I cannot venture far, I will learn. Look how many more books there are in the world!*

And with that thought came memories of Corinthia's library tour.

So. Many. Books.

The scrub jays called out encouragement, for they were a curious bunch who loved trouble. Between the scrub jays and the forest, it was all Rosemary could do to keep the lot of them in line.

She planted the makeshift walking stick into the sand. "We will take it slowly," she repeated, for the benefit of everything listening—and herself.

All beings present heard, and at least one did not obey.

15

A long session of forest bathing, followed by a more civilized walk with Beaufort, followed by an ice-cold shower, should have been a recipe for a restful evening. But even a cup of cocoa laced with cardamom and Ceylon cinnamon, plus a pile of new books from the library, couldn't settle Corinthia for bed that night.

She tossed. She turned. She got up and sat on the couch, annoyed. There was so much advice on how to fall asleep, and not a bit of it worked: Turn off your devices. Reduce your blue light exposure. Make your bedroom dark and quiet. Exercise, but not too close to bedtime. Go to bed at the same time every night and get up at the same time every morning. Don't have coffee after lunch, or, preferably, at all; and definitely don't nap.

Corinthia had done it all, and was thoroughly convinced that those who dispensed this advice had never experienced insomnia, and were just making wild guesses based on what *sounded* helpful, because none of it was *actually* helpful.

Beaufort, who had looked up from his living room cozy spot when Corinthia huffed ino the living room, sighed and closed his eyes again.

What a lovely sleep Corinthia had after Rosemary stopped by. Where were mysterious, sleep-inducing women when you needed them?

Corinthia got up. Beaufort followed. They both stepped onto the back porch.

Beaufort was quiet, even solemn; his nose twitched for scents on the night air, and its moist, textured surface reflected moonlight.

There was an outdoor couch on the screened porch. Corinthia hadn't used it much, preferring the air-conditioned atmosphere inside the house—but something about it, on this night, in this light, made it look appealing in a way it never had before. Perhaps she might curl up on it, rest for a short time; let the novelty of the nighttime outdoors trick her mind into sleepiness.

Sensibly, though, with a pile of blankets and a real, hon-est-to-goodness bed pillow.

She retreated, leaving the door open for Beaufort to come and go, and gathered the necessary bedding. She heaped and arranged the pillows and blankets on the outdoor couch, leaving aside one of the more tattered but still serviceable blankets for the dog, who liked to make a nest of it on the floor.

When Beaufort had finished inspecting the porch and the night air, he turned several circles and settled contentedly on the blanket. His eyes watched, then drifted closed, then opened again as something Corinthia could not see mildly caught the hound's attention.

Corinthia felt fully awake—foolish, even—as she struggled to fit her legs on the couch and get herself fully covered without any drafts creeping through gaps in the blankets. "This is silly," she said, to an audience of the dog, and whatever bird was hooting quietly in a nearby tree, "I'm obviously not going to fall asleep. I'm going to get a book."

And so she disturbed her own carefully-made nest of blankets and went inside to retrieve *Alien Space Lesbians* and a clip-on reading light. She settled in once more.

Other sounds faded as Corinthia was swept into the void of space, and, by proxy, into the arms of the alien space lesbian—who seemed to be highly competent at many things,

from spaceship piloting to engine repair and fine motor control. Corinthia approved.

The moon peered through the highest branches, and thin, glowing clouds sped across the sky in a wind that didn't reach the ground.

Small things moved in the yard, overturning leaves and bending blades of grass one at a time.

And beyond, the Refuge swayed, hypnotically.

Beaufort breathed gentle puffs of air, his puppyish contentment seemingly catching.

"Silly," Corinthia repeated, her eyes closing, her voice in her own ears sounding as if it came from as far away as the spaceship, as she slipped into a dream of white sand and twisted trees.

It was some time later when the noise came that would have woken anyone.

CRACK.

Corinthia started. Her eyes opened. Her blood rushed as if she had nearly fallen and had only caught herself just in time. Woozy and confused, it took several seconds to remember where she was and how she had gotten there in the first place.

Corinthia groaned softly and stretched her stiff limbs. How long had she been asleep?

And what had made that terrible noise?

The book lay on the floor, its pages woefully bent. Corinthia scooped it up and smoothed the pages.

Beaufort was already alert, his nose held high. He let out a clarion bay.

"Hush!" Corinthia said. Even the most laid-back of neighbors could be driven to confrontation if woken in the middle of the night. "Hush, Beaufort! People are trying to sleep." Corinthia set the injured book aside, pushed herself upward, and rubbed her eyes. Only then, with full clarity of sight, did she realize exactly what had caused the loud cracking noise.

The back fence. Its posts lay flat, cracked at the bases like cheap toothpicks.

The support beams Drew had so carefully installed had been flung outward like javelins, except for a few that were snapped in half if they had not been thrown clear.

The pickets and rails lay on the grass like the beginnings of a new deck. And, as if to add insult to injury, the white sand of the Refuge had been sprinkled over everything like sea salt on a bar of dark chocolate.

All of the work, all of it, smashed to bits in one moment. The fence lay defeated.

Corinthia, who did not believe in barefoot walking under any circumstances, flung off the blankets. Cold concrete slapped the bottoms of her feet. She slipped out the screen door and stepped off the porch. Chilled sand infiltrated the spaces between her toes. Damp grass left cool trails of moisture along the side of her feet; she felt it all but ignored it, rushing across the lawn.

She walked onto the platform of the fallen fence and stood in the breach itself, the surrounding tree limbs black like the sky, the underlying sand white like the moon.

Again, the neighbors' fences stood untouched. But this time, a new path had opened up. It unfurled like a snowy carpet into the interior of the Refuge before disappearing, as such paths seemed to do, around a corner.

Corinthia looked back at her little house. Despite its closeness, it seemed to have moved farther away. The yellow lights in the windows shone brightly but distantly. Beaufort could be heard pawing at the screen door, no doubt worried why his mistress was on the other side at a time when all should be tucked up in bed.

Corinthia looked down at the border between her home and the Refuge, reduced to a literal line in the sand: where the fence lay, and beyond it. She swayed; in the darkness her balance was not what it should have been, and to look down was like balancing at the edge of a steep cliff and feeling gravity's pull to what lay below.

This was the time to turn back. Morning was the proper, sensible time for dealing with such things.

And yet the pull was there. The pull of the Refuge, that had set its burrs into her heart the day of that ridiculous bet with Stevie, and now refused to set her free.

"Don't be silly," Corinthia said to herself, against the strong suspicion that she had already been quite silly, in one way or another, and that *that* had somehow led to *this*, in a way she did not fully understand. In rebellion against this fear, she brought one foot firmly to the ground outside the fence—and gasped.

The whole world shook. Deliciously. And personally—just as the neighboring fences were untouched, Corinthia was certain that only she had felt Shadow Ridge rock on its axis.

On second thought, perhaps Beaufort, too. Dogs were wiser than most people gave them credit for.

Corinthia looked into the deep, dark woods. The breeze that finally touched the trees made the leaves shift, which, in the cool light, looked like many eyes blinking back at her.

In all of Corinthia's life, almost everything could be found in a book, comfortably folded in the gift wrap of its cover and the snug padding of its pages. And if that were true, as Corinthia knew it to be, then this, too, could be explained. She was ready to solve it. Ready to understand. A librarian's need to catalog could not be withstood.

She turned her back on the Refuge and strode across the lawn. Entered the porch. Called the dog to heel. Walked inside and carefully dried her feet before putting on regular clothes, a pair of fresh socks, and her walking sneakers. She generously sprinkled Beaufort's bed with treats to encourage him to settle down and rest.

And then Corinthia went outside, shut and locked the door, and returned to where her fence lost its battle with the Refuge.

She placed one foot over the border and felt the world tremble, which only made her more determined to understand, to find what unknown process knocked down fences and made the Refuge bloom in her mind like wildflowers, uncontrolled and beautiful.

She stepped fully inside.

Her eyes adjusted slowly. What had at first appeared to be impenetrable darkness revealed itself one plant at a time, resolving into full clarity: oak trunks becoming visible beneath the branches; flowers acquiring light on their blooms; lichen revealing its shape. Though everything should have been tending to drowsiness, the Refuge had never seemed more alive.

When the trees knocked against each other, it was not unlike when the elementary school students set up their wooden xylophones for a show in the outdoor amphitheater, and nervously tapped the keys while waiting for instructions from the teacher.

Even the birds sounded excited. They surrounded Corinthia invisibly, to the left and right and ahead, their cries casting a joyful net around her. They were welcoming her, she thought, and immediately chased the thought away for its sheer absurdity.

She walked on, slowly, certain that whatever had trounced her fence must reveal itself if she paid close enough attention. She reached the turn in the path and looked back. Moments ago it had looked far away; now it looked like a house she had once lived in, long ago. Not hers at all but something that had moved on without her, or that she had left behind.

She turned the corner.

Suddenly the comparison to Castle Adventure was no longer whimsical but almost literal. The walls of the path stretched a little higher, grew a little thicker. When she wasn't looking at them directly she could have sworn there were small pinpricks of light within, like will o' the wisps.

Corinthia wished for high ground—for turrets like the old Castle Adventure, to see down into the maze. Pizza and birthday cake would have been nice, too. Chocolate cake with chocolate frosting.

She continued down the path. There were no landmarks to be seen. She had walked several of the trails, yet did not recognize this one, nor how it might connect to the others. It was no longer a surprise that Stevie had gotten lost even after working here so many years.

Corinthia drifted along, as if in a dream, footsteps quiet on the cool white sand, quiet enough to hear a soft hiss of movement behind her. She looked back to see the gray snake minding its own business and crossing the trail, tongue flickering in a thoughtful and utterly nonthreatening way.

The Corinthia who would have run split away from the Corinthia who did not, and disappeared, like a ghost, into the past.

Corinthia of the present nodded briefly to the snake, as if to a colleague, and kept walking.

The lights in the tangled oaks grew brighter, like old-fashioned gaslamps turned up to a higher flame. At this level of illumination it was surprising that the residents of the surrounding neighborhoods did not descend on the Refuge out of curiosity—but then, Corinthia had lived in such a neighborhood for years, and had never seen anything out of the ordinary.

She could only assume that whatever was happening here was only visible here. Or only visible at certain times, or to certain people. She could not be sure. Corinthia thought of herself as many things—librarian, chocolate lover, dog rescuer, friend—but had never conceived of herself as someone who would be the exception to a rule.

A scrub jay appeared on the path ahead. It was small, and pretty, and almost inexplicably sassy, and it kept hopping forward and looking back as if to see if Corinthia would follow.

For once, she listened to her instincts and did not shove them into darkness like overdue books in a return box. If she could accept the existence of unusual fence-smashings and lighted maze-forests, why resist a bird with a personality? Corinthia followed the bird.

When the incline finally increased, Corinthia took the hill with long strides, eager to reach the top. She would get her bearings. She would understand, finally, and never be troubled again by falling fences or nonsense in general.

She reached the top, turned a corner, and at last gained a clear view into the Refuge below.

And what she saw... made absolutely, positively, no sense at all.

16

The first part of the view made sense. The path down the hill unfurled like a white carpet. At the bottom lay the larger of the two Ephemeral Wetlands, gemlike and shining, surrounded by tall pine trees. It was what was beneath the trees, beside the water, that made no sense.

A house, deep in the heart of the Refuge.

A little house, on a small rise, with tidy walls made of hedges and a roof thatched from living branches. There were two window-like openings on either side of a round-top door crafted of skinny oak trunks twisted tightly together.

Lupine, shiny blueberry, and lyonia grew in neat flower beds beneath the windows, and a path of dried pine straw led up to the door. The night wind brought the scents of pine, water, and flowers to Corinthia.

In a way, the house reminded her of home: a woodland twin, as small and simple as her own—and yet, all of it was impossible.

For a house to stand near one of the Ephemeral Wetlands was definitely impossible; Corinthia would have run smack into it, or at least glimpsed it, on one of her rambles. No one lived in the Refuge.

And yet, there it was. A green mansion. Or a green cottage, to be precise—snug and glowing and surrounded by tended patches of flowers.

This was wonderment beyond the ordinary, beyond what had ever existed in her range of experience up to that point, expanding over the border of normal and into the sublime. Her curiosity had woken like an animal from hibernation, stretching and taking its first tentative steps in a changed world.

Still not quite believing her eyes, Corinthia took out her phone. A perfectly acceptable phone camera should have been enough to capture the basic outlines of a house, even in the dark. As she pressed the shutter button, Corinthia suffered a split-second panic that the mere act of photographing the green cottage would make it disappear.

It did not disappear, but as far as the photo was concerned, it might as well have. Just as the Refuge had lost its depth in the daytime when recorded in two dimensions, so too did the shape of the house lose all definition. The picture looked like bushes that, perhaps, if you squinted, *might* have been a house—if you had a vivid imagination.

Corinthia surveyed the Refuge from her high vantage point. None of the paths looked like they had before. Like Castle Adventure, it seemed the maze had shifted. Venturing downward meant entering the unknown.

Was it possible to be both cautious and brave?

From below her came a flutter of wings. The scrub jay landed on the path down the hill and looked up at her expectantly. Then it cocked its head, pivoted, and hopped downhill, as if it had already decided that Corinthia would follow. In faint illumination the scrub jay was more silver than blue, washed out into the monochromatic shades of an old silver tea service.

She could at least be as brave as a scrub jay, Corinthia thought. So she followed the bird down the hill, attempting (in case anyone was watching) to look strong and unafraid. It worked quite well until she tripped on an exposed root and stumbled down the last of the incline and into the clearing.

The bird flew to the ledge of one of the windows, and without further ado, fluttered inside and was lost to sight.

Corinthia faced the house alone, a trick-or-treater with no costume or candy bucket. Heat lighting silently billowed through distant clouds, lighting them up from the inside.

So much had happened. It was a strange sensation, then, to feel as if even seemingly insignificant events had been leading, inexorably, to this moment: Drew's book selection, the lost wallet, the words of Mr. Thriller during the panel, her spur-of-the-moment decision to sleep on the porch. Each was another step in the maze.

Now she was here, and there was a door before her. She told herself it wasn't too late to turn back, to walk home, to pretend nothing had happened; to crawl into her own bed, in her own safe little house, and resolve never to set foot in the Refuge again. But just as she could not resist turning pages to find out what happened next, she could not resist knowing what might lie behind that door.

She took the last few steps across soft, dry pine straw, and knocked.

The surface of the door was uneven, being made of living and entwined branches, and felt rough on Corinthia's knuckles. In case the muted knocking was not heard, Corinthia added her voice. "Hello?"

There was a rustling sound inside.

The door cracked open. Golden light shone through the opening and dazzled Corinthia's vision into a moment of spangled blindness. She raised her hand to shield her eyes, and then the glow silhouetted someone with graceful, sweeping lines.

Rosemary stepped fully into the doorway.

Oh, Corinthia thought, *it's you*. Because of course it was.

Rosemary wore the now-familiar blue and silver-gray silk, tied into a fetching sarong-style dress which showed her arms to best effect. A slightly crumpled hat of dark blue straw completed the look. Ah, but where were the gemstones that always adorned Rosemary's outfits? Corinthia's gaze traveled until she found them, in a jeweled brooch on the hatband.

Stars twinkled. Frogs croaked in the Ephemeral Wetland. Lupine stems trembled.

What could Corinthia say? *I see you live in the Refuge? Love what you've done with the place?* There were ways of talking to people—procedures that could be followed—and very few of them applied in this situation. When she finally gathered her wits to speak, she said, "You look like an island princess," and was so shocked that these were the words that had fallen out of her mouth that she actually laughed out loud at herself.

Rosemary laughed, too. "In this old thing?"

"I am *so* sorry," Corinthia said, hiding her face with her hands. "I don't know what's wrong with me."

"Nothing is wrong with you," Rosemary insisted, pulling Corinthia's hands away from her face and holding them in her own. "Would you like to come inside?"

"Is it... is it *real*?" Corinthia had a brief vision of the whole thing disappearing, and then waking up on her back porch, victim of a dream within a dream.

"Oh, it's real. It's just shy."

"Your house is *shy*?"

"With strangers."

"Am I a stranger?"

"Not anymore."

One of the only things Corinthia could be quite sure of was that this simple welcome felt like a cool glass of chocolate milk, fulfilling a thirst she didn't know she had. She had always loved to know things, but had never fully considered the pleasure of *being* known.

Rosemary stepped back and held the door open.

Corinthia was about to cross the threshold when a question suddenly occurred to her. "Where'd the bird go?"

Rosemary's eyes widened. "The bird?"

"Yes, I saw it fly through the window a minute ago."

"Oh, *birds*. They act like they own the place. Come in, come in."

The question went unanswered, but Corinthia went in.

In one corner, branches framed a cozy bed that appeared to be made with fluffy lichen and flowers. Another tangle of branches resolved into a chair padded with thick, soft-looking grass. A pine stump served as a side table. The walls of the cottage, however, contained the real show-stopper: rows upon rows of books, marching along branch and vine shelves that appeared to grow organically from the walls.

Fashion Through the Ages. Emily Post's Etiquette. The Art of Dancing. The Complete Book of Herbal Medicine. Dozens of Harlequin titles. A history of Elizabethan England. A tattered but complete Jane Austen collection. Rows of vintage cookbooks. Airport thrillers and obsolete New Age tomes and everything in between.

It was as if the contents of the free book cart had been carefully collected and shelved over the course of years. Come to think of it—Corinthia scanned the books with a well-trained eye—there was the *Introduction to Woodworking* she herself had put on the cart! She looked at Rosemary. "You took all of them?"

"Maybe not all..."

Corinthia raised her eyebrows.

"A lot of them," Rosemary admitted. "But I trade them in when I'm done. Otherwise I'd run out of space."

A whole education, Corinthia thought. "How long have you lived here?"

Rosemary turned away, industriously straightening up one of the living, leaf-dappled shelves without answering the question, so Corinthia retreated to a previous topic. "Your collection is amazing," she said. "I can't believe you put it together entirely from the free book cart."

"Everything but *Alien Space Lesbians*. That one I had to get from the library proper."

Corinthia, who was not good at being nonchalant, went for it anyway: "Was there—uh—any particular reason you wanted that one?"

"Because I wanted to read about women in love, and you don't get that kind of thing on the free book cart too often."

"Oh," Corinthia said, releasing a breath she had held without thinking. *Oh.* A sweet happiness rose in her soul, like waking up and realizing a book you've been waiting to read for years has finally been released.

"Do *you* like to read about women in love?" Rosemary asked.

Corinthia nodded vigorously. Oh, *yes*, she did.

"Someday," Rosemary continued, airily, "I shall meet a wonderful, beautiful, bookish woman, and I shall promptly fall for her. Especially if she is slightly grumpy and has trouble expressing her feelings."

This was such a wonderful thing to hear that Corinthia could have heated a mug of cocoa simply by pressing it to her own cheeks, and it took her a full minute of recovery to notice that there was something missing in the green cottage.

The green cottage had no kitchen.

Even as new to the Refuge as Corinthia was, she had learned quite quickly that there was little to nothing in it that could sustain a person. Pine needles to nibble, certainly; and wild blueberries here and there for a few months; but no *food*, not in the quantity needed to survive.

If there was no kitchen then how did Rosemary eat? Where was the food? How would she not waste away to nothing?

"Rosemary," she said, taking the direct route, as it was the one she knew best, "what do you eat out here?"

"I had some of your chocolate," Rosemary said, not meeting Corinthia's gaze.

"Rosemary," Corinthia repeated, affectionately severe, "you can't survive on the occasional chocolate."

Rosemary looked up from her shelf-straightening. "You care!" she said.

"Of course I care," Corithia replied, trying to sound gruff but, by the amusement on Rosemary's face, failing entirely. This was the third time, by Corinthia's count, that Rosemary had left a question unanswered, or changed the subject, but Corinthia could be patient.

Once, she had gone out to walk in the Refuge and got caught at the picnic pavilion by a sudden downpour before she could enter the trails. Distant lightning snapped across the sky and thunder rumbled in its wake. She sat in the shelter and watched the rain fall on two slow-moving box turtles for a good twenty minutes. Then, all at once, the clouds flew apart and revealed the blue sky.

"I'm being a terrible host," Rosemary said, hurrying over to the chair crafted of living woven branches and vines, and tuft-ed with fresh-growing green grass. She gave it a pat. "Would you like to sit down?"

"I can't take your only chair."

"I'll make another. We'll sit together—won't that be nice?"

Corinthia took in the sturdy, beautiful shelves; the hand-made, herbed, and flowered bed; and fully believed that Rosemary could grow a chair on command.

Even if she seemed to be doing it in part to avoid answering questions.

How long had Rosemary lived here? How did she eat? And where *was* that bird, anyway?

Corinthia carefully lowered herself into the chair, as if it might not hold her weight, but it cradled her like the most finely engineered ergonomic chair, and she relaxed into its support. She did not have to be quick with words, now. Rosemary had a whole chair to grow, and Corinthia had time to think. Overthinking could be her greatest weakness, it was true. But its more sensible cousin, plain old *thinking*, was her greatest strength.

Rosemary stood by the pine stump side table next to Corinthia's chair. She closed her eyes, breathed deeply, fidgeted slightly as if getting out a small case of the wiggles, then held her hands in the air, palm-down, as if she might play an invisible piano.

A moonlight glow surrounded Rosemary's hands. It slowly enveloped her arms, then her entire body, until she was haloed with soft silver light. Corinthia's exposed skin warmed from the gentle radiance.

Rosemary breathed again, seeming to draw upon something Corinthia could not see but could, in a distant way, *feel*—like the far-off thunder outside.

And then there were little plants growing out of the pine straw floor, reaching upward; twisting and turning and coming together and splitting apart; bursting out in bright green leaves all over; reaching and climbing as if they competed in a joyful race to grow taller, all while spinning the scent of spring into the air. They wove together and settled at last into the familiar shape of a chair, all-over puffy with fresh green grass.

Rosemary opened her eyes and smiled. Corinthia clapped appreciatively. Rosemary curtsied, then sat, with a sigh of relief, in the new-grown chair.

"Was that tiring?" Corinthia asked.

"A little," Rosemary admitted. "But it's good for practice." She settled more comfortably, and appeared to be thinking.

Corinthia sat quietly. It was something a librarian knew how to do.

"I must seem secretive to you," Rosemary said.

"We are all secretive about certain things." Corinthia reached out to Rosemary, and for a few moments, they held hands without moving or speaking, the gulf between them bridged by simple human contact. "Don't be afraid,"

Corinthia said. Those eyes of midnight stars watched her as she spoke. "I know what it is to be different."

"Do you?" A hint of a smile passed over Rosemary's lips, as fast as clouds over the moon. "I believe that you do," she said. "Come outside with me. I have something to show you."

They stood in the clearing in front of the snug cottage, where the ground was cushioned by dry, fallen pine needles. Lightning was not close, but it was close enough to scatter flashes of white light across the water in the Ephemeral Wetland.

"Stand back a little," Rosemary said.

Corinthia took a few steps back, careful not to trip over a fallen branch or tangle herself in the long stalks of grass. If went too far and fell in the water, it would be Rosemary's turn to fish her out.

The night noises harmonized: wind in the trees, sleepy doves deep in the underbrush, leaves falling on water. Rosemary raised her arms, and it looked like she might conduct a chorus.

From all around came the cries of scrub jays. One by one they appeared at the tops of the trees, like small shadows trimmed out in paper by a silhouette maker, until it seemed every scrub jay in the Refuge had converged around the Ephemeral Wetland.

She's summoning the birds, Corinthia thought.

And then, one by one, the birds descended.

They perched on Rosemary's outstretched arms. On her bare shoulders. On her straw hat with its jeweled brooch. All the while they murmured and chirped, and when they ran out of room on Rosemary herself, they landed at her feet like feathered courtiers around a queen.

A queen with a rumpled straw hat, topped with a single scrub jay with an endearingly worried expression.

Rosemary held steady and looked Corinthia in the eye. "This," she said, "is my family."

At first, Corinthia could think of nothing to say to this. There were no established social guidelines for responding to someone who thought their family was a flock of rare birds. But because she had seen more of the unexplainable in the last week than most people see in a lifetime, she did her best to improvise. "What do you mean? Do you take care of them?"

Rosemary chuckled and shook her head. The bird on her hat flapped its wings and hung on. "If anything, they take care of me." She paused. "I'm... one of them."

Surely she meant "one of them," as in one of God's creatures. This was an acceptable metaphor, Corinthia concluded, which anyone could conceivably use. "You're... one of them?"

"I'm a bird, Corinthia."

I'm a bird.

The acceptable metaphor shattered.

The three words repeated in Corinthia's mind—*I'm a bird, I'm a bird, I'm a bird*—as if the words themselves were a bird call.

But this person was clearly not a bird. This person was—strange, special, beautiful, *magic*, even, but a human being with arms and legs and a straw hat. Not a bird.

I found the perfect woman, Corinthia mused, *and she thinks she's a bird.*

And yet...

There were things she did not understand, but had discovered to be as real as anything mundane. Corinthia knew she was convincing herself and still she did not stop: A forest had reached for her as she slept and knocked down her fence. An author had been lost and found. A hidden house had grown in the forest. If those were real, then why not this?

"I would show you," Rosemary said, "but it doesn't work that way. I can't transform in front of a human."

Of course not, Corinthia thought.

"Do you believe me?" Rosemary said, her sweet voice filled with hope.

There had been stories about shapeshifting women for as long as stories had been told. Whether Rosemary had learned them or lived them, Corinthia did not know. *Humor her*, she decided, *and maybe it's true*. "Of course I do," Corinthia said. "No wonder you said your family doesn't drink alcohol."

"Well," Rosemary said, "unless the blueberries ferment. Then you might see a few drunk birds."

Corinthia laughed. She didn't need to believe in magic, but she desperately wanted to believe in Rosemary.

Rosemary glanced at the dozens of birds around her. "I've gotten them up past their bedtime. I'd better let them go." The scrub jays fluttered away. The last to go was the one from her hat, and then the two of them were left alone in the clearing. "Now you know why I don't need food or a kitchen," Rosemary said. "I eat like a bird, literally."

"You just transform to eat."

"Yes, exactly."

Corinthia nodded. Sure, why not?

"And don't worry," Rosemary added. "I have the lifespan of a human, not a bird. Or at least I'm pretty sure I do, considering how old I am now."

Corinthia did not know it was possible to feel relief and disbelief at the same time, but the two feelings sat side by side like books on a shelf. "I'm glad to hear that," she said.

"I used to stay in bird form most of the time, but the older I get, the more time I spend like this."

Corinthia nodded some more. Nodding was easy to do.

"When I was a bird I would perch in the trees above the Pollinator Garden for storytime, and then I would become a human to sneak over to the free book cart. Then it was back to bird form to watch TV over back fences." Rosemary smiled. "You don't know how wonderful it is to finally *tell* someone!"

Corinthia smiled back. It was impossible not to, because Rosemary was kind and lovely and clever, and really, who cared if she thought she was a scrub jay? Thinking you're a bird is a quirk, not a dealbreaker.

"You don't think less of me, do you?" Rosemary asked. She cast a rueful look at her own sarong, and one elegant hand touched her hat self-consciously. "All my clothes are blue and gray, like my feathers."

"They're beautiful," Corinthia said, with complete sincerity, though she was not sure whether she meant clothes or feathers or both. "But we could go shopping somewhere, if you wanted something different..."

"Oh, but I can't! I have a very hard time leaving the Refuge."

Stevie had once pointed out how the scrub jays never left the Refuge, and Corinthia had filed it away as an interesting bit of trivia about scrub jay behavior. Now that the woman standing in front of her had applied this bit of trivia to herself, it seemed much more pertinent. Was it a phobia? Or something wrapped up in the idea of believing she was a bird? Or was she truly a bird, with a bird's instincts? "You really can't leave?" Corinthia asked. "What happens if you try?"

"I can go a little way—to the library, or just outside the border of the Refuge, but after that it's difficult. I feel all wrong and anxious."

"Maybe if you practiced, it would become easier."

"Do you think it would?" Rosemary said. "I would love to see more of the world."

There were things Corinthia had to say, and to say them she needed to be closer to Rosemary. She closed the distance and met Rosemary's gaze. "Listen," Corinthia said, "I don't care if you eat acorns in your spare time. It doesn't bother me if you spend half your days in feathers. I want to understand what is happening to me in this forest. The things I can do; the things *you* can do."

Corinthia went on. "You want to get better at leaving the forest. I want to get better at"—she made a wordless gesture for *all of this*. "We can help each other. It would be..." Corinthia paused, searching for sensible, rational, convincing words, the kind that would have convinced her if she were on the receiving end. "Mutually beneficial," she concluded.

"Mutually beneficial," Rosemary echoed, her eyes wide and solemn.

"It would require spending time together," Corinthia added, gravely.

"Lots of time," Rosemary agreed, equally serious.

"Extensive conversations, outings, that sort of thing."

"Oh, yes."

"Are you teasing me?"

"Definitely," Rosemary said, her eyes sparkling. "In fact, we should start tonight."

"Tonight?"

"Yes, tonight! *Now* is always the best time!"

"Some of us," Corinthia said, trying to be stern, "have to work in the morning."

"I *know*," Rosemary said, with great sincerity, as she drew Corinthia toward the green cottage. "You don't have to stay up. You can just sleep over!"

"How would we have a conversation if we're asleep?" Corinthia stopped short. "Also, I am *not* sleeping in the woods."

"Not the woods," Rosemary said, coaxing her onward. "A lovely bed of soft moss and flowers. Remember how I helped you sleep before?"

"Yes—how did you do that, by the way?"

"Stay and find out."

"Not until you explain to me why sleeping in the woods would be at all helpful."

"The more time you spend in the forest," Rosemary said, "the more you will understand."

"Even asleep?"

"Even asleep."

Corinthia found herself at the doorway of the green cottage, hidden lights twinkling in the foliage like fireflies, torn between long-established habits of home and the excitement of something new. "I'd have to get up in time to go home and get ready for work," she said. But it was only a few hours until daylight, anyway. Beaufort would be sleeping peacefully, dreaming doggy dreams. The practicalities were a permission slip, and Corinthia knew it, but she pursued them anyway because practicalities brought familiarity and comfort to new situations. "You really think it will help?"

"Yes," Rosemary replied, very seriously.

Above them, the sky grumbled, and sent its warning shot in the form of scattered raindrops. The lightning seemed closer than before, as if the weather itself would make the decision on Corinthia's behalf.

Who said nature didn't have a sense of humor?

"I have to inspect the bed," Corinthia said, brushing raindrops from her hair. "I'm very particular."

Rosemary hurried inside and Corinthia followed.

"For your approval," Rosemary said, patting the green, fluffy surface of the bed. "One-hundred-percent pure, dry moss, over an elevated support surface of entwined branches, and finished with accents of dried herbs and flowers."

"You sound like a mattress ad."

"I watch TV from back fences, remember?"

"Hmph," Corinthia said. "Blankets?"

Rosemary reached into a cubby Corinthia hadn't noticed before. She fished out a large, thick tartan blanket. "Ta-da!"

"That is not a magic forest blanket. You stole that."

"I borrowed it."

"From a laundry line."

"And a very nice laundry line it was, too. I'll put it back," Rosemary said, spreading it over the bed and folding back one edge. "Someday."

Corinthia snorted.

"Lie down," Rosemary said.

"For a bird, you're very commanding."

"Scrub jays are bossy." Rosemary steered her to sit.

Corinthia allowed herself to be directed, pausing only to remove her shoes. She reclined on the moss, which was heaped up at one end for a pillow-like effect, and immediately her nose filled with the herbal scent.

Rosemary covered her with the blanket. She placed her indigo straw hat on the living bedpost, then carefully crawled into bed beside Corinthia. The bed was small enough so that Corinthia's hip pressed softly against Rosemary's.

Rosemary brought her hand up and delicately stroked Corinthia's forehead and temples.

It was all very snug.

It had been a long time since Corinthia had shared a bed with anyone, and yet she found that she preferred this simple tenderness over any more earthy pleasure she had previously experienced. She relaxed into the moss, closed her eyes, and allowed herself to be soothed. "How did you do it before?" she asked, her voice already beginning to sound drowsy.

"Do what?"

"Make me fall asleep."

Rosemary was silent, in a peaceful way that seemed to mean that she was thinking about what to say. Rain pelted the trees outside, but couldn't find its way into the cottage or under the warm tartan blanket. "You have trouble sleeping when you're not close enough to the forest," she said. "I just brought the forest to you."

"Is that what happened to my fence? The forest decided to get a little closer?" Corinthia said, dreamily, feeling a delicious frisson race through her.

"The forest gets excited about meeting new people."

Corinthia chuckled. "Do you?"

"Do I what?"

"Do you get excited about meeting new people?"

"Yes." Rosemary had turned her head toward Corinthia to answer, for Corinthia could feel the warmth of Rosemary's breath on her neck. "Especially librarians who read *Alien Space Lesbians*."

With that, Corinthia smiled, and whatever grip she had on consciousness loosened. She was beneath the roof of a green cottage, tucked under a warm blanket, beside a bird-woman; and whatever dreams might be whispered in her ear as she slept, she wanted them all.

18

In the morning, Corinthia drifted into awareness of the early sunlight; the weight of the blanket; the scent of greenery all around; and finally, the warmth of Rosemary, peacefully asleep beside her. She had been dreaming of building a nest, cozy and sturdy, piece by carefully placed piece.

Corinthia turned her head, trying not to make noise, knowing that Rosemary woke early and wanting to claim these remaining quiet moments to gaze at her face without the self-conscious fear of being observed.

Corinthia could not remember when she had first noticed the cupid's bow shape of Rosemary's lips. Now, in the slowly gathering light, they looked more perfect than ever. A fondness rose in Corinthia that felt like it was not new; it felt like it had been there forever, a dormant seed awakened at last with the proper application of water and time.

Rosemary stirred.

Corinthia carefully slid out of the green bed and replaced the blanket where she had been, to hold in the warmth. Upon inspection of her handiwork, she decided to tuck the blanket a little more firmly around Rosemary as well.

"Corinthia," Rosemary murmured.

"Ssh," Corinthia said. "Go back to sleep. We'll meet again later, okay?"

Rosemary's eyes remained closed but she smiled and nestled deeper into the bed. "Okay."

Corinthia brushed a few bits of moss from her clothes, stepped into her shoes, and took one more look around.

It was all unbelievable, the kind of thing you could never tell anyone, for fear they would think you unwell or a liar.

Corinthia knew she would tell Stevie straightaway.

She opened the door, which did not creak but swung silently on its living hinges, and then closed it behind her. With the cottage at her back the Refuge could have been the same as it ever was, only now she knew one of its secrets, and she was poised to learn more. The thought, like a stack of new, unread books, was thrilling.

And Rosemary needed help. This filled Corinthia with purpose, a potent motivator, for there was nothing more Corinthia loved more than to be loosed in a direction like an arrow from a bow. She could be of so much service, if given a bit of time to think and make lists.

She set off up the hill.

After sleeping in the Refuge she noticed a new sense of direction. She had only to think of a place—the small Ephemeral Wetland, an unusual formation of trees, that patch of wild blueberries—and a silvery sense of it immediately arose in her mind, showing the way. It was the same sense she had noticed on the day of the local author festival, only now it was clearer and more in her command.

Home, she thought, and knew the path instantly.

The morning light turned from silver to gold as she made her way through the Refuge.

Around one last curve she spotted her own fence, like a drawbridge lowered into her own backyard. She walked across the wooden slats and stepped down onto the grass. She crossed the remaining turf and opened her back door to find good old Beaufort still in bed.

The hound raised his head and his tail whipped back and forth. He stood up and stretched a deep, doggy stretch, front paws extended all the way forward.

"You will not believe the night I've had, Beaufort." Beaufort trotted over for pats and behind-the-ear scratches. Corinthia obliged. "Let me use the bathroom, my friend, and I'll get you outside for a walk."

When she returned, she bent down to put on the dog's harness and leash, wondering if the green cottage had its own facilities, or if Rosemary changed into a bird like she did to eat and drink. It might make long stays awkward if Corinthia had to walk all the way home for a restroom.

Long stays! Corinthia straightened up with the leash in hand, Beaufort pulling at the other end. How could she even be thinking about long stays? They had known each other for a few days! Yet as quickly as the practical side of Corinthia called out this issue, the practical side of Corinthia also brushed it aside by deciding that Rosemary would have to come to Corinthia's place for long stays, if necessary. Problem solved.

More pressing, in the light of day, was the problem of how she could casually accept the existence of someone who claimed to be both bird and woman.

Because, she concluded, *it is as likely as anything else.* If the world could contain green cottages with living timbers, it could certainly contain bird-women.

And that was that. She took Beaufort outside.

But what to *do* with Rosemary? If she was like the scrub jays—if she *was* a scrub jay—then Corinthia must learn more about scrub jay habits. Rosemary deserved to be free as... well, a bird!

Where could she go that was close to the Refuge? There was the Shadow Ridge Library, of course, and the Shadow Ridge Environmental Center; the Pollinator Garden, and the Outdoor Amphitheater. The parking lot was more distant but not by much, and it had the pop-up vendor fair.

On the other side of the Refuge was Corinthia's own neighborhood. Rosemary had already proven herself able to cross that border well enough to reach Corinthia's house. Perhaps she could reach Stevie's house, if she tried.

When Corinthia returned to her front yard, her home's resemblance to the green cottage struck her fully: also green, petite in size, simple in its lines, with a barely-used kitchen and shelves upon shelves of books.

Beaufort, however, was not interested in such things, and instead applied his nose to sniffing the grass as if he had never sniffed it before in his life.

"Beaufort," Corinthia said, "what do you make of all of it?"

Though the hound had been known to ignore her entirely in favor of the pursuit of a scent, Beaufort lifted his head so quickly that one ear flipped backward. He looked at Corinthia with knowing eyes, then shuffled over and leaned his flank against Corinthia's shin.

Corinthia softly turned the dog's silky ear down and smoothed it into place. "You probably know everything," Corinthia said. "You just can't say it."

Beaufort huffed.

"Come along, dog." Corinthia led Beaufort back inside, where he was thoroughly patted, treated, fed, and watered before Corinthia left for the Shadow Ridge Library.

She managed not to spill anything to Stevie other than to ask to meet for lunch in the Pollinator Garden. Work flew by when it should have dragged. Corinthia pushed the free book cart outside with even more vigor than normal. She processed books and shelved books and found books for patrons. She had such a renewed sense of purpose that even the lights in the artificial tree seemed to spark with new meaning.

At lunchtime, she took her bagged lunch to the Pollinator Garden and sat on the bench beneath the arbor, facing a trellis covered with yellow-flowered vines. Makeshift bird baths here and there reflected the cloudy sky, and stepping stone paths wound through plantings of milkweed and bee balm. The plant containers didn't match, either, which added to the lively garden chaos. A touch of informality, Corinthia reflected, made a space more welcoming to newcomers.

Curious scrub jays bravely ventured a few feet out of the Refuge and drank from the bird baths, vigilantly looking all around between beakfuls of water. Corinthia peered at them, looking for signs that one of them might be Rosemary, but other than the distinctly alert eyes they all possessed, she could find no feature with which to firmly identify the woman with whom she'd spent the night.

There were other species of birds, too. Occasionally they would squabble amongst themselves. Their noisy calls made the garden slightly less tranquil than one might have imagined, and sometimes gave it the air of a winged boxing match.

Stevie approached on the outer path, ponytail rampant, lunch bag swinging.

Corinthia waved.

Stevie plopped down on the bench. "So!" she said, elbowing Corinthia. "You had something to tell me?"

Corinthia opened her brown paper bag, took out a peanut butter sandwich, and began to unwrap it.

"Well?" Stevie prodded.

"I'm thinking," Corinthia said.

Stevie, who was well-used to Corinthia thinking, took out her own lunch container and opened it, revealing segmented compartments of cheese, meat, fruit, and veggies, along with a separate space for dip and another spot for M&Ms.

"I went to Rosemary's house."

Stevie abandoned the baby carrot she had been about to bite. "You *what*? Where does she live? And how did you end up there?"

"I slept there."

Stevie's mouth fell open.

"Not like you think. She helped me sleep again."

"I'll bet she did—"

"*Not like you think.*"

Stevie shrugged and traded her carrot stick for a chunk of cheese.

Satisfied that her beloved but altogether overheated friend was done insinuating, Corinthia continued. "She lives here."

"At the library?"

"In the Refuge." And before the questions could begin, Corinthia told the entire story, from her late night on the back porch, to the fallen fence, all the way to the green cottage, the bird conclave, and the mossy bed.

"But I've never seen a green cottage," Stevie protested, when Corinthia was done.

"No one has," Corinthia said. "I think that's the point. It's hidden."

"I feel left out, frankly. All these years, and none of the birds turned into a human and slept with me. Why you?"

Corinthia shrugged.

"I know why," Stevie said. "Because she *likes* you."

"Don't start."

"And you like her, too."

"By the way, have you asked Drew on a date yet?" Corinthia said, changing the subject with more blunt power than finesse.

"Of course I have... not," Stevie said, poking at the M&Ms like they might do something interesting.

Corinthia sighed.

"We're hopeless," Stevie agreed.

"Stevie," Corinthia said. "You need to stop batting your eyelashes and just ask Drew on a date."

"What if she says no?"

"What if the sun becomes a red giant and engulfs the Earth?"

"Dark—but okay, point taken."

"How about the next concert at the Outdoor Amphitheater? I'll ask Rosemary to come, too," Corinthia added.

"Are you asking her on a *date*?"

"I'm helping her get used to being outside the Refuge."

"Oh, that's a new one."

"Look, if what she says is true, all she knows of people is what she's learned from discarded books, passing hikers, and bits of TV. She has to take this at her own pace. I can't go... *wooing* this person."

"Fine, you're not 'wooing' anyone. You're bringing her to a concert minus the *woo*."

"Thank you," Corinthia said, stealing an M&M. "But how do you invite a rare bird to a concert?"

"Practice your birdcalls. Leave a trail of birdseed. No—wait," Stevie said. "Use your spiffy new magic powers."

"I could just walk to the green cottage at night."

"Too easy. Where's the fun in that?"

"You just want to see me accidentally magic my own hair off or something." Corinthia held out her hand. "More M&Ms, please."

Stevie doled out a few. "Why don't you have your own chocolate?"

"Rosemary ate most of it. I haven't refilled the auxiliary Cabinet of Chocolate yet."

"There's your answer, then. Summon her up, offer her some chocolate and a concert, and she'll fall at your feet."

"First of all, I'm not 'summoning' a fellow human being—"

"Bird-being."

"Second, I don't *want* her to fall at my feet. I want her to accompany me, by choice and with dignity, to a cultural event."

Stevie rolled her eyes.

"But... the rest of your theory is solid."

"So you're gonna work some of that magic?"

"I," Corinthia said, with more calm than she really felt, "am going to leave a message with the forest."

19

The Pollinator Garden bordered the Refuge, so after lunch it was easy enough to follow one of the sand paths down a slope, through a gap in the low fence, and into the outermost fringe of the Refuge itself.

A secondary trail, not marked on the map, led quickly into a stand of thick, impenetrably tangled oaks, their green walls rising on either side of the path and blocking the view of anything but the cloudy sky above.

"I need a likely tree," Corinthia said.

"A likely tree," Stevie echoed, running her hands over various branches as if shopping for the perfect 7-foot Christmas spruce. She stopped and looked at Corinthia. "What constitutes 'a likely tree,' anyway?"

"I'll know it when I see it." As silly as it sounded, it was absolutely true. Self-assurance was beginning to take root in Corinthia, as if she had begun to put to use a new technology she had been learning about. How different was this, after all, than a Boolean search? Or a card catalog, from back in the day?

"Just close your eyes," Corinthia said to herself, remembering the forest bathing instructor, "and hold out your hands, and *feel*, until you notice something."

There was only the steady pressure of her feet on the ground, the rustle of the leaves, and the subtle scent of floral, smoky honey in the air. Even with her eyes closed there was a visual sense of silvery energy woven through everything, occasionally brightening in spots like tiny sparks.

Corinthia had done some more reading about the flora and fauna of the upland forest, and had learned that some oak trees interconnected their roots with their neighbors, forming a strong, linked community that did not fall even in hurricane-force winds. Rosemary's tidy green cottage was just as much a part of it as the stand of trees in which Corinthia stood.

"Corinthia?" Stevie said.

"I've got it," Corinthia said, and smiled to herself, because she did, indeed, have it. Every fiber of her had been linked to this place, and she felt the movement of the trees like her own fingers wiggling. She touched one of the oak branches, but it was almost a formality—a way to show respect and willingness.

I would like to invite Rosemary to the concert tonight at the Outdoor Amphitheater.

Her words became images wrapped in memories and feelings, and Corinthia released them into a network she was only beginning to understand. A vibration passed outward, echoed off the farthest reaches of the Refuge, and returned to her in pulsing shivers. Goosebumps rose on her arms.

Corinthia opened her eyes.

"Did you do it?" Stevie said.

Corinthia nodded.

"Did she—uh—write back?"

Corinthia let go of the branch and stood silently. The forest was silent, too. She had almost opened her mouth to say "no" to Stevie when a rush of silver began at the outermost range of her senses and rolled toward her like an ocean wave, bright with metallic spray.

It reached her from every direction at once: an enthusiastic *yes* from the trees, from the wind, from the sand beneath her feet. It was through the forest but not *of* the forest; it was Rosemary in every sense.

"She said yes," Corinthia said.

Stevie pumped her fist into the air.

"Your turn," Corinthia prompted, nodding toward Stevie's pocket where her phone would be.

"Oh, right!" Stevie plunged her hand into her pocket and removed her phone. She raised it and waggled it in Corinthia's direction. "At least with Drew, I only have to send a text message."

That evening, when Corinthia had gone home to wash up and dress, she faced her closet with the coolness of mind of someone who was unsure about a great many things, but not clothing. It had taken years to determine what she liked and what she wore well, and once she had, she simply replicated the concept over and over, replacing like with like whenever anything wore out.

Everyday clothing she didn't fuss about much. She had library t-shirts for work, and for any exercise she might take, a pair of track pants and an old t-shirt suited her fine.

But for an outing, she broke out the good stuff: nice jeans, a crisp white dress shirt, a tailored blazer. Special sneakers she kept in tip-top condition for dressy occasions. A flashy pair of gold earrings—hoops or something dangly—and, if she was really feeling foxy, a hat to top it all off.

Tonight, a black fedora.

"What do you think, Beaufort?" she said, holding her hands out and turning in a slow circle.

Beaufort thought this was a marvelous new game and leaped as high as he could, trying to reach the treats he imagined were waiting in Corinthia's outstretched hands.

Corinthia stopped turning, grabbed a handful of treats, and ran the hound through all of his known tricks until her phone dinged insistently, one text after another in quick succession. Stevie had sent four shots of the same outfit from different angles.

Stevie's going-out fashion also differed significantly from her daily look. No more khaki shorts and a nature-related t-shirt. Stevie glowed in an off-white jumpsuit and strappy sandal flats, hair let down from its usual ponytail to dance around her shoulders, a gold-toned lariat necklace and cuff-style bracelets adding glitz and color. Her makeup continued the golden theme with a wash of shimmery highlights. *Is it too much?* Stevie wrote. *I don't know what Drew will be wearing.*

You look great, Corinthia wrote back.

Do you think she'll like it?

If she has any sense, Corinthia wrote. She tucked the phone in her inside jacket pocket, did one last check of Beaufort's supplies—food, water, toys, blanket—picked up a ribbon-tied box she'd placed on the counter, and left her car in the driveway in favor of going out the back door and over the makeshift drawbridge her fence had become.

The instant she set her foot on the sand, it was like coming home; like opening the door to a place she had loved all her life, though she had only really known of it for a few days. Her heart felt like a compass—the green cottage, true north—and she followed the path eagerly, pausing only at the top of the tall hill to smooth her lapels and carefully adjust the fedora to its most flattering angle.

Down the hill, the branches waved a greeting in the evening breeze, and the hidden birds alerted one another like old-timey newsboys shouting, "Extra! Extra!"

Corinthia looked at the box in her hand and wondered, like Stevie had about her outfit, if it was too much. Maybe the ribbon was too much. She pulled it off, felt foolish, and tied it back on again. She had picked these bonbons one by one, just as she would have curated a display of books: thoughtfully, with an expert eye.

Yes, chocolate was a perfectly acceptable gift. People gave one another chocolate all the time; ask anyone. Corinthia hurried down the hill, forgot the tree root, and tripped just like she had before.

At least she didn't drop the chocolate.

The sky had faded down to the last haze of pink along the western horizon. The trees were almost silhouettes, except where they were close, in which case their leaves took on a silvery sheen. At first the cottage was not visible. There was only a heap of shrubs, wider than they were tall, marking the place where it had been, and Corinthia had a brief moment of panic when it became possible that she had imagined all of it.

But when she stopped at the bottom of the hill, what had not been there moments before immediately resolved itself, as if something had been quickly focused, like a microfiche machine, and there was the little green cottage with its round top door, two windows, and flowerbeds. All around the forest began to glow with its warm points of light, and the same illumination permeated the cottage walls and roof, until everything around the clearing was beautifully and comfortably lit.

Before Corinthia could even approach, the door sprang open and Rosemary ran outside, arms outstretched. "You came!" She closed the distance, and before Corinthia could think, let alone dodge, Rosemary wrapped her arms around her in a kinetic hug that almost tipped Corinthia off balance.

"Well, hello to you as well," Corinthia said, one arm pinned to her side, but the other arm managing to pat Rosemary on the back with the box of chocolates. "I brought snacks."

This got her an extra squeeze before Rosemary released her. "You did? Oh, you shouldn't have," Rosemary said, immediately setting to work at pulling the ribbon off the box and removing the lid.

It gave Corinthia time to finally get a look at what Rosemary was wearing: a snug, short, curve-fitting dress of ruched blue and silver-gray silk, snazzy as a cocktail dress, with a matching cape that reached to the hem of the dress. Corinthia willingly played the game of finding the jewels that always embellished Rosemary's outfits. Where were they? At the clasp of the cape, setting off the outfit to perfection.

To stand there, in her best jacket and hat, next to this angelic person, made Corinthia feel like she was on the way to the prom. Instead of balloon arches there were twisting oak branches; instead of a photo backdrop there was a bower of lyonia shrubs. Fireflies lit the pine straw dance floor and crickets and frogs served as disc jockeys.

It struck Corinthia that though a bird may never have been to a school dance, Corinthia really hadn't either, not in the way she had wanted to; not with a girl. Times were different, then.

They would step out together, forest prom queens at last.

Rosemary's quick and graceful fingers plucked a bon bon from the box. "You must have the first one."

"No, really, I—" But Rosemary was pressing it to her lips and what was Corinthia to do but eat the whole thing in one bite. It was one of the chocolate-covered cherries; her favorite. "Mm," she hummed, through the confection.

"Pick one for me," Rosemary said, her eyes flashing anticipation.

What could she pick for a bird-woman unversed in chocolate candies? Her fingers hovered indecisively before selecting the remaining chocolate-covered cherry. She held it out.

Rosemary tilted her head back a little bit and opened her mouth. Apparently it was still possible to make a mischievous face while your mouth was open that wide.

Corinthia put aside thoughts of birds in the nest and popped the chocolate into Rosemary's mouth. She could tell the moment the cherry liqueur burst, because Rosemary's eyes closed and she made a noise of delight.

"This," she said, after swallowing, "is the greatest present ever."

"It's nothing, really." Corinthia found herself looking down at her feet, not quite able to be the object of so much praise but also nearly glowing with it at the same time. "Would you like to put it inside before we go?"

"I suppose we can't stuff ourselves with it at the concert?"

"We could if you wanted to. It's not formal; they have a concession stand with candy bars and popcorn and everything."

Rosemary looked torn, to the point where she looked down at the box, back up at Corinthia, and down again. Finally she took the box and reverently put the lid in place. "We will save it for after," she said.

A thrill passed through Corinthia at the idea of "after."

She watched Rosemary walk swiftly to put the chocolates inside the cottage. Such neat and economical movements she had! Quick and precise, yet naturally graceful, accented by the fluttering short cape that now reminded Corinthia of wings.

She had so many questions. But it was enough that they were in this place together, and when Rosemary emerged, it was *all* that mattered. There were no questions that couldn't be answered by Rosemary's smile.

"You look so pretty," Rosemary said.

It was so completely without art, as genuine as the fresh air, that Corinthia could not help but feel the surprise manifest on her own face, and was caught flat-footed without an immediate response.

"I have seen you before," Rosemary continued, "in other things—just as nice!—but there is something different about you tonight."

"Thank you," Corinthia said, and they walked on, down the path that led north to the library complex. "I thought it would be good to dress up. Your outfits are always so stylish."

"Oh, this old thing," Rosemary said, with a modesty that vanished when she did a little spin, making the cape fly.

"You can wear other things, though, right? Like the night at the library, when you fell in the pond?"

Rosemary chuckled. "I can. But I must always keep this with me," she said, brushing at the shoulders of the cape. "Or else I cannot change form."

"Like a swan maiden," Corinthia said. She had brushed up on shapeshifting folktales.

In the distance, the musicians began to warm up. The crickets responded in kind. A few disrespectful birds shouted criticisms. Clouds passed over the moon, dimming the moonlight, but the glow in the forest seemed to compensate by twinkling more brightly.

There were more sounds nearby—rustling, clicking, croaking—that would have startled Corinthia before, but now only made her want to put an arm around Rosemary to shield her from any reptiles or bugs who would dare to crash their dark forest walk. Whether this was motivated by protectiveness or a secret desire to snuggle, Corinthia was unsure, but she was perfectly content to ignore the question entirely.

Overhead, Sagittarius took aim at the half moon. If he loosed an arrow, it would break the perfect lunar black-and-white cookie in two.

One half for me, one half for Rosemary, Corinthia thought.

20

As they approached the Outdoor Amphitheater, it could have been just another hill rising out of the Refuge, but as they drew closer it sculpted itself into a shell-like structure with semi-circular rows radiating upward from the stage.

By the time they entered, many of the tiered seats were taken. People stood on the steps, chatting, or wandered around with snacks in hand, looking for the best view of the stage below. Between the voices and the warming-up instruments and the rattle of the nearby trees in the evening wind, it was louder than Corinthia remembered.

But Rosemary had slipped her arm through Corinthia's, and because of this, Corinthia would have been fully content to stay there until the sun rose.

Then Rosemary waved happily at someone down in the seats.

"Corinthia!" Stevie called across the din. "We're down here!"

Corinthia waved back, pressed her fedora on more securely, and proceeded with Rosemary down the steps to join Stevie and Drew, who had saved space for them.

Stevie, resplendent in gold, beamed under the lights. Drew, with her natural coolness upgraded by a black leather jacket over a black tank, accented by a silver star pendant, greeted them with her usual chin lift—plus a friendly handshake for Rosemary, who seemed pleased by everything.

Once they were settled, Stevie and Drew began to chat with one other. It was a perfect opportunity to engage Rosemary, but Corinthia found herself staring out at the stage, unable to come up with a single thing to say. She looked around, discarding conversational ideas as fast as she could think of them, until she saw a family passing a bucket of popcorn back and forth. "Would you like some popcorn?"

"Oh!" Rosemary said, seemingly enthused by the idea—but she quickly subsided, adding, "No, I'm all right." Her usually impeccable posture wilted ever so slightly.

Why had she turned it down? Corinthia thought fast. Rosemary had no money of her own, and if she had said yes, it would have put Corinthia in the position of having to pay, and—oh, of course she turned it down! Corinthia could have slapped her own forehead. She should have just bought some snacks and given Rosemary her pick of things, as she had done with the chocolates, and now she had messed it all up.

Could she text Stevie and ask her to buy popcorn for all of them? That would work, but she was having such a nice conversation with Drew...

No, she would have to solve this herself.

"I'll trade you some popcorn," Corinthia said, "for a favor."

Rosemary met her gaze, her expression lifting prettily.

"If," Corinthia said, putting on her best librarian voice, the quiet-yet-firm one that had quelled rowdy teenagers at twenty paces, "you will teach me how you grew that chair in your cottage."

"That sounds very fair," Rosemary replied.

"All right, then," said Corinthia, who was trying to be serious but got thrown completely when Rosemary put an arm around her shoulders for an affectionate squeeze, followed by what seemed to be a little snuggle. She finally managed to gather her wits, stand up, and stagger up the stairs to the concession stand, where, in a daze, she ordered a whole lot of popcorn.

She carried the four red-and-white cardboard containers back down, spilling only a few bright yellow pieces like wedding confetti, and briskly handed them to her friend, her friend's date, and Rosemary. She seated herself again and began munching contemplatively, less out of hunger than as an excuse to sit quietly for a few moments and not have to say anything clever.

Rosemary plucked at the popcorn pieces, eating one at a time, neatly, with precision.

"Do you like it?" Corinthia asked, wondering if bird-Rosemary had already eaten popcorn, and if it tasted different in human form, and whether she should look up whether popcorn was good for birds, just in case.

"Crunchy," Rosemary said, thoughtfully. "Puffy."

"And salty," Corinthia added, eating a few more, then noticing Rosemary's gaze on her. "What?"

"There's one stuck on your shirt."

"Where?" Corinthia whacked at her crisp white shirt, looking desperately for the offending corn and wishing she'd bought a less messy snack.

"Hold *still*, Corinthia," Rosemary chided, amusement all over her face.

Corinthia stilled. Rosemary reached over—clever fingers grazing a pearl button, which caused Corinthia to inexplicably break out in a sweat—and plucked a small piece of popcorn from where it had gotten lodged under the point of Corinthia's collar.

"You're welcome," Rosemary said, and then tossed the popcorn in her mouth, crunching demurely behind a self-satisfied smile.

Corinthia was outright relieved that the overhead lights dimmed, leaving them in partial darkness, because she did not like to be seen to be flustered. And Rosemary, with her smiles and her company and her green cottage and her magic, had flustered the living daylights out of Corinthia.

As the musicians raised their instruments and struck the opening notes, Corinthia realized that her feelings toward Rosemary were spilling over like the trees of the Refuge in her backyard, knocking down the fence she had carefully reinforced.

It didn't matter that Rosemary thought she was a bird. Or, alternatively: that Rosemary *was in fact a bird*. Or that she lived in a magical cottage no one else could see. It wouldn't be the first time a woman had an unconventional identity or living situation. Those who truly cared would understand—and those who did not, were not owed an explanation.

Corinthia sat a little taller and looked around the venue.

A handful of couples were using the top level of the amphitheater as an impromptu dance floor. They were joined by an assortment of small children, who had less polished moves but exuberance to spare.

Corinthia found herself smiling at the sight. The Refuge, the amphitheater, the music and dancing—all of it seemed so right that it was as if a flower of rightness was blooming right there in her chest, next to her heart, its petals fluttering with every beat.

Rosemary patted her hand.

Corinthia looked at her, questioningly.

Rosemary took her hand and slipped into the aisle staircase, tugging Corinthia after her.

With a surprised backwards glance at Stevie, who shooed her off encouragingly, Corinthia went up the steps behind Rosemary.

They reached the top level and faced each other, in their own little space. Corinthia would have loved to impress by leading the dance, but improvisation was not—to say the least—her strong point.

Rosemary's gaze went to a nearby couple whose salsa moves were smooth but simple. She watched, nodded to herself, then held out her hands to Corinthia.

Corinthia fixed her fedora firmly and took Rosemary's hands.

They began to move, hesitantly at first, but gaining in sureness with each step, back and forth, back and forth, until confidence strengthened Corinthia's daring and she let go with one hand, spinning Rosemary away decisively with the other.

Rosemary spun, throwing her head back and laughing as she did so.

When they joined both hands again, something light and quicksilver flashed through Corinthia. Where there was music, there was also birdsong; the trees waved their arms in the air; in the sky, distant stars strobed.

Something was happening. Something was changing. She felt it everywhere, but especially where her fingers touched Rosemary's.

Corinthia had an idea. "Come back with me after the show," she said.

"Back where?"

"To my cottage!"

Rosemary smiled her assent.

When the song ended, everyone applauded the musicians. Rosemary curtsied extravagantly to Corinthia, and Corinthia swept off her hat and bowed.

The night was not yet over.

21

After the concert ended, and Stevie and Drew had wandered off to discover whatever might still be open in Shadow Ridge, Corinthia accompanied Rosemary out of the amphitheater and down to the sidewalk on the edge of the parking lot.

Rosemary had wanted to practice leaving the Refuge.

"I would love to travel," she said, gazing out at the parking lot as if it were the first step on a long journey.

"How far have you gone before?"

"In this direction? Only to this sidewalk."

There were cars pulling out and driving away into the night. Their headlights swept across the bordering trees like spotlights. "Whenever you're ready," Corinthia said.

"I'm ready," Rosemary said. She hesitated. "Could I ask you to hold my hand?"

"You don't even need to ask." Corinthia's hand enveloped Rosemary's, which was warm and soft.

They stepped down from the sidewalk. At first their pace was normal, but as they approached the third row of parking spaces, Rosemary slowed.

"Are you all right?" Corinthia asked.

"Yes," Rosemary said, although she was noticeably breathing harder, and her face had taken on a look of determination.

Corinthia squeezed her hand, and they walked on.

They passed the third row.

"It's very hard now," Rosemary admitted.

"We don't have to go on—"

"One more row."

Corinthia could tell that Rosemary was pushing herself the extra distance, and respected her all the more for it.

They reached the fourth row.

Rosemary exhaled. "I think this is as far as I can go today," she said. She looked down at the ground. "I feel silly. I should be able to go anywhere, and here I am taking two steps in a parking lot."

The embarrassment in Rosemary's voice melted Corinthia like chocolate on a s'more. "You did *great*," she said. "You can't help your nature."

"And now you have to walk all the way back to your place, too—"

"I could use the exercise," Corinthia said, firmly. She would not let this woman berate herself; not a chance.

They held hands all the way back to the winding path that traced the exterior of the Outdoor Amphitheater, and only let go when they descended into the Refuge.

As the bright spotlights faded behind them, the haunting call of an owl floated through the darkness. Corinthia noticed things she had never seen before, like a gopher burrow dug out of the sand, and the glittery eyes of spiders hidden in the scrub. Nothing was perfectly safe, but everything was beautiful in its own way.

At the top of a rise they stopped to watch the orange moon burn its way above the horizon.

"I've never seen it like this," Corinthia said.

"You never spent enough time in the forest," Rosemary replied. She chuckled. "And I've never spent enough time out of it."

"We are a pair, aren't we." The words left Corinthia's lips before she could second-guess them into extinction.

Rosemary didn't seem to mind the implication. "We are," she said.

Overhead a chain of lights twinkled past the planet Jupiter. Though Corinthia knew the lights were only a line of low-orbit satellites, it was more fun to imagine them as spaceships piloted by lovelorn aliens.

Back on earth, the fireflies glowed on and off.

Corinthia and Rosemary continued through the twisting pathways, Corinthia following the beacon of her home as she sensed it on the southern edge of the Refuge. They walked companionably in peaceful silence, which the night overlaid with its own harmonies.

To feel Rosemary moving through the trees; to track the alighting of her gaze on one thing or another; this was better than chocolate, Corinthia concluded.

When they reached her backyard, Corinthia offered her hand for Rosemary to step up to the unintended deck made by the wooden fence.

They stepped down to the sandy soil again on the other side.

The backyard was plain as it had ever been, with only sand, patchy grass, and the one lone grapefruit tree, planted when the house was built and hanging on as best it could. Corinthia loved the fruit tree but grieved that the whole lot had been cleared just to leave empty sand and boring grass in its place.

"Do you think," Corinthia said, "that we could regrow the forest here?"

"We could," Rosemary replied. "If that's what you want."

"I do. I have to put the fence back, for practical reasons—"

"Good old Beaufort," Rosemary said.

"Good old Beaufort," Corinthia agreed, "but there's no reason the forest can't have a little more space. It's the least I can give. And it's not like I use the yard for anything but the dog. To be honest, I would tear down the whole house and grow one from living trees if it wouldn't attract too much attention."

"You're a romantic," Rosemary observed.

"I'm practical. It's eco-friendly."

"Be honest," Rosemary teased. "You want a magical cottage, too."

"All right, fine. I want a magical cottage. I admit it."

Rosemary laughed.

"I feel silly for penning myself up indoors all the time," Corinthia added.

"You didn't sit out here and read?"

"I should have. But I hardly spent any time out here, until I fell asleep on the porch the other night."

"A little forest," Rosemary mused, gliding across the lawn, "a few chairs; a little table, for beverages—hot cocoa?—a blanket, for warmth..."

"Yes. Yes!" Corinthia said, warming to the idea. "I have some things I can bring outside."

"I can see it now," Rosemary said.

The two of them shared a look filled with happy, imaginative thoughts.

"I saw you grow that chair," Corinthia said, closing the distance, "and I knew I could do it too. I just knew."

"I know you can," Rosemary said, fervently. "Come. Let's do it now! It's dark, and no one will see."

"What do I do? How do I start?"

"I'll help you. Let's face the forest."

Corinthia turned north.

Rosemary moved behind her and wrapped her arms comfortably around Corinthia's waist

Corinthia felt Rosemary's radiant warmth against her back, and it was a struggle to stand up straight, and not lean back into the cradle of Rosemary's embrace.

"It's okay," Rosemary said. "You can relax."

"I'm not good at relaxing." Corinthia exhaled, intentionally, letting herself go softer, more supported, placing her hands on Rosemary's where they lay softly on her belly.

"Are you ready?" Rosemary murmured.

The words were so close they fluttered Corinthia's pulse. "Ready."

Despite the cool air, Corinthia felt warm all over, until it felt as if she breathed magic, sending motes spinning through the air like mist after a long, hot shower. A glow blossomed around their hands, then slowly made its way up their arms before enveloping them both entirely in what looked like a haze of moonlight.

Their bodies were trunks and branches; their hair, leaves unfurling. They were the forest and the forest was them. Beneath their feet raced new roots, filament-fine but expanding, tracing through the sand like silver electricity before new growth broke ground and reached toward the sky.

There were oaks, and lyonia bushes, and wild blueberries, and with each new growth the backyard became wilder until Corinthia and Rosemary stood surrounded by a new stand of trees, shrubs, and smaller plants, the first of their kind to grow in this patch of land in generations.

"More," Corinthia said, and felt Rosemary's answering smile without having to see.

They drew deeply, calling on the aquifer beneath their feet. More plants blossomed—tiny flowers on stalks like hatpins; bushes of bell-shaped flowers; shrubs bursting with strange, peanut-shaped fruit.

And then more trees grew from beneath the fence, pushing it upright until it stood as if it had never fallen, trunks growing tight against the boards, living vines lashing it into place and decorating it with large, purple-edged flowers that faded to a creamy yellow center.

"Satisfied?" Rosemary said.

Corinthia's whole being rang with magic. She didn't want to stop, not ever, and could no longer see why pulling down her own house and growing a green cottage over it was a bad idea, until she remembered her beloved Beaufort nestled in his bed. So she held onto Rosemary but let go of the earth, the water, and the silvery haze that had, for a moment, made her forget herself.

They stood, basking in the new-made forest together. A pair of birds swooped in from the outside forest, curious to see what all the fuss was about, and landed out of sight with a sweet, whistling song.

Rosemary rested her head on Corinthia's shoulder. She swayed once, twice.

Corinthia, alarmed, turned and caught a half-swooning Rosemary in her arms. "Are you all right?"

"I'm fine," Rosemary said, dreamily. "Just a little tired."

Corinthia bore her up, one arm firmly around Rosemary's waist, allowing Rosemary to lean against her as she guided their steps. Her backyard, so unremarkable before, now had tiny white sand paths through the low, twisted trees; a Castle Adventure in miniature.

It was a bit of a trick to open the screen door and get the drowsy Rosemary through it, but Corinthia managed. Years of pushing carts and carrying heavy books seemed to have strengthened her in all the right places.

One more door, into the kitchen, and there they were with Beaufort, who presumably did not know that he had nearly had his house replaced by a forest. He sniffed curiously around their ankles, galloped alongside as Corinthia maneuvered Rosemary into the living room, and then watched as she lifted her head at last and gazed happily at the papasan chair.

"Oh, look!" she said. "It's a nest within a nest." She walked unsteadily across the room, plopped into the papasan cushion, and curled her legs up. Her hands pillowed her head and her eyes closed.

Beaufort, ever the gentleman, hauled himself into the chair, back legs paddling briefly into the air before he worked his way comfortably into the crook of Rosemary's legs. He laid his head peacefully on the side of her knee and looked at Corinthia with satisfaction.

Corinthia looked at the two of them. Who would have thought?

She took a blanket and pillow from the linen closet. She tucked the pillow under Rosemary's head, gently moving her hands aside. She laid the blanket over Rosemary, leaving Beaufort uncovered. She hesitated, then carefully undid the clasp that held Rosemary's cape closed, and loosened the cape from around her neck. Then she smoothed back the strands of hair that came loose.

Rosemary smiled in her sleep.

Corinthia stole a closer look at the metalwork and gems on the clasp. For the first time, she noticed that the leaves and flowers shaped into the design were all plants from the Refuge. If Rosemary was only telling a story about her true nature, it was the most beautiful fabrication Corinthia had ever encountered.

She carefully tucked in the blanket and left the bird-woman to her dreams.

22

The smell of hot food woke Corinthia the next morning. She opened her eyes to the golden light of the Saturday sun, the sound of the television, and something sizzling. Who could be cooking? Not Rosemary, certainly. She had no kitchen and no experience. The whole kitchen could be aflame in moments!

Corinthia threw off the covers and hurried out of her bedroom, her dream of flying alongside a scrub jay rapidly fading into the reality of the day.

A cooking show played on the living room television. Outside, in what had previously been a grass and sand backyard, stood a chunk of forest, bright green in its newness.

In the kitchen, Rosemary stood over the stove, turner in hand, while Beaufort stood sentry a respectful distance away just in case anything edible hit the floor. His tail whipped back and forth in a hopeful manner.

"You're up!" Rosemary said, waving hello with the turner. Her hair was pinned up cleverly with jeweled combs, and it was almost unfair how cute she could look in one of Corinthia's dress shirts—stolen, jauntily tied at the waist to reveal a bit of belly—and a pair of shorts that might have been denim if Corinthia didn't already know for sure they were a beautiful approximation made from blue-gray silk.

Corinthia came to a stop. "Are you... cooking?"

"I watched a TV show."

Corinthia moved closer. Yellow scrambled eggs nestled in the hot pan, just a tick of the clock away from being fully set. "But you've never cooked before..."

"I'm a quick study."

The corvid family, Corinthia had learned—which included crows, ravens, and jays—was indeed known to be extremely intelligent. "Let me help you."

"Sit down," Rosemary said. "You're always giving me your best chocolate. This is the least I can do."

Corinthia, unaccustomed to taking orders or being idle in her own kitchen, did not move. She didn't *intend* not to move; it was as if someone had planted her deeply in one spot and she could not figure out how to get herself free.

Rosemary smiled indulgently. "Sit, Corinthia." She placed her hands on Corinthia's shoulders and bodily steered her to a seat at the kitchen table.

Corinthia began to rise from the chair. "But you're my guest—"

Rosemary tapped Corinthia's nose, which made Corinthia go briefly cross-eyed and had the effect of knocking her back into her seat. "Now, where's your juicer?" Rosemary began flinging open cabinets.

"Juicer?" Corinthia had not juiced anything in years; nor did she, to her knowledge, have anything in the refrigerator or pantry that could be considered juiceable.

"Never mind!" Rosemary brandished a small, manual juicer triumphantly.

"But we don't have anything to juice—"

"Ta-da!" Rosemary held up oranges that had been hidden from view in the strainer, in the sink.

"Where did you get those?"

"Your neighbor's tree."

"You stole oranges from my neighbor?"

"*Stole* is such a strong word."

"What would you call it?"

"Liberated."

Corinthia couldn't help laughing. "You learned all this from one cooking show?"

"I told you, I'm a fast learner," Rosemary said. She expertly halved and began juicing the oranges. "Plus, I've been watching TV for years over back fences, remember?"

"I remember." Corinthia watched her work—how clean and economical her movements were—and wondered what the odds were, out of all the galaxies in the universe, with their hundreds of billions of stars, that she, Corinthia, would be the one to have such a person cooking her breakfast. "Do you have plans for today?"

"Breakfast," Rosemary said, sensibly. "Why?"

Beaufort looked at Corinthia, as if to say, *Go on, then*.

Corinthia tried to be nonchalant, but the words came out in a bit of a rush anyway: "If you're not busy, Stevie was going to bring over her new electric scooter and we were going to take turns trying it out. Unless you have something to do, of course."

"What I have to do," Rosemary said, sliding the hot eggs out of the pan and onto two plates, "is learn how to ride an electric scooter." The toast popped—she snagged it and dealt it like cards. Finally, she poured two small cups of orange juice.

Now I can help, Corinthia thought triumphantly, rising from her seat. She took the plates and Rosemary carried the cups.

Beaufort ambled hopefully alongside as they carried everything to the table, then sat on his haunches next to the table and looked soulfully upward, his usual method for convincing visitors to share.

Seated with the simple, fresh breakfast between them, Corinthia and Rosemary traded shy looks before digging in. Rosemary's fork technique was at first unsteady, but her natural grace soon brought it into alignment with the highest standard of table manners.

Corinthia cleared her throat. "Last night was really something." She hated to be so imprecise, but what were the right words for what she had experienced? "Are you okay, by the way? You nearly swooned on me."

"Sorry about the fainting," Rosemary said. She lightened the words with a smile. "I'm used to magic for one, not two."

"Did you sleep well? I was worried the papasan chair wouldn't be comfortable, but I didn't want to try to move you once you settled."

"Where would you have moved me?" Rosemary replied, playfully.

"Anywhere you wanted to be." Corinthia would have given Rosemary the bed, if she had so desired, and repaired to the couch like a good host. She stopped short of imagining anything more familiar, because Corinthia was well-practiced at self-denial of everything except chocolate and books. "I was so tired I almost got carried away and knocked down my own house, but for Beaufort." Corinthia nodded toward the dog, whose ears perked up at the mention.

"I wouldn't have let you. I like your little house. You shouldn't knock it down."

"All I could think about was more room for the Refuge."

"Did you know about the other plot of land across the street?"

Corinthia did not.

"There's another section that was set aside but never managed. If it was added on, it could expand the Refuge by half over."

Corinthia laid down her fork. "I did not know that." There were so many things she had not known. For so long, she had let her domain be the library, and the library alone. She had always thought, in a way, that the Refuge was Stevie's purview. But no more: Corinthia vowed to herself to steward books and nature, nature and books, as if the two had never been separate at all.

The light from the north-facing windows lay coolly on Rosemary like a wedding veil, soft and blue-white. "You're staring at me," Rosemary said, not unamused.

"Sorry," Corinthia said, looking down and fumbling her knife at the same time, sending a chunk of egg tumbling to the floor.

Beaufort lunged at the speed of delight and quickly slurped the egg bit, leaving the tile floor licked clean. Clean for a dog, that is.

Before long, Beaufort settled down for an after-breakfast nap and Stevie was knocking at the front door. The three of them went down to the end of the driveway, and luckily, the street was completely empty of cars.

"Who wants to go first?" Stevie said, maneuvering the electric scooter into position.

"Me!" Rosemary said. She reached eagerly for the handles.

"You don't think the distance will bother you?" Corinthia asked.

Rosemary eyed the street, calculating something only she could perceive. "Your street runs right alongside the Refuge. I should be fine as long as I don't turn on a side street."

There was a bit of a shuffle as Rosemary removed her jeweled combs and put them in her pockets, and Stevie helped her put on, buckle, and tighten the helmet. In almost no time at all, Rosemary stood with helmet on, one foot on the scooter, one foot on the ground, posture straight as a dancer.

Stevie explained the controls one last time and stepped back.

With a whir of the motor, Rosemary took off, buzzing down the street, her borrowed shirt flapping in the wind. "Woo-hoo!" she cried, the sound rapidly fading as she sped away.

"She's got a knack," Stevie said.

Rosemary had zoomed out of sight.

"Stevie," Corinthia said. "I don't know what to do."

"About riding a scooter?"

"About *her*."

"Tell old bestie Stevie about it."

"I *like* her."

"Of course you do. She's very likeable."

"You know what I mean."

"You mean, *like* like. As if we were in middle school."

"You're no help at all." The scooter buzzed in the distance and Corinthia acutely felt the passage of time before Rosemary would be standing in front of her again. "I don't know how to tell her properly."

"The twelve-hour dates and sleepovers weren't communicating it? Chocolate delivery and breakfast at your place not getting the message across?"

"I don't want her to feel obligated—"

"Obligated!"

"Yes, obligated! Just because she seems to have some affection for me and I seem to be the first human she's really gotten to know, doesn't mean she has to fall in love with me. I don't want to put her in the position of feeling like she owes me anything."

"Corinthia," Stevie said, solemnly. "You're too stuffy for your own good."

"Maybe I am. But I care for her whether she feels the same way about me or not. If she were never to look my way again I'd still think of her and wish her well. She's... special." Saying it out loud loosened something in Corinthia, something that made her fearful and brave all at the same time. "I want to protect her."

"Then use your words and tell her how you feel."

"I'm not good at that."

Rosemary zoomed toward them, face aglow, wind-stung cheeks rounded with happiness, and Corinthia had to stop herself from diving into a hedge to hide.

Stevie applauded as Rosemary stopped on a dime and dismounted with a hop. "You're a natural!"

Rosemary curtsied. "Thank you," she said. "It's just like flying!"

"Corinthia, why don't you go for a ride with Rosemary?"

"Oh, no," Corinthia said. "I'll throw off her balance."

"Nonsense!" Rosemary said. "I'm stronger than you think. Get on!"

"I don't have a helmet—"

"I won't crash. Here, get behind me and put your arms around me."

"Yes, put your arms around her," Stevie said, who was not above shamelessly egging all of this on.

Corinthia stood carefully on the back of the scooter and slipped her arms around Rosemary. Because the scooter deck was not very long, she had to hold on quite tightly to fit. She had rested in a bed with Rosemary and had not been this close, this snug, this all-encompassingly pressed against her, warm and soft and firm in all the right places, smelling of forest and fresh air and sun-warmed flowers.

"Ready?" Rosemary said.

Corinthia, who was having trouble forming words, managed to reply something affirmative, and off they went.

At first her stomach jolted from the fast start, but when the acceleration smoothed out she had to admit that it did feel like flying—and terror, too, if she was honest, because she wasn't a thrill ride kind of person; didn't care for motorcycles, or roller coasters, or carnival rides of any sort—but this thrill was something altogether unrelated to speed, though it shared with it a feeling of uncontrolled adrenaline. Her arms, around Rosemary; two heartbeats flying in unison.

23

Later, after they had zipped up and down the street to their hearts' content, Rosemary decided to go home and have a rest. Corinthia would have liked to follow, to perhaps catch a glimpse—or not—of an avian transformation, but good manners prohibited sneaking around in such a way. Besides, she cared for Rosemary far too much to seriously think of making her uncomfortable. So Corinthia and Stevie stayed out front of the house long enough for Rosemary to make her way through the backyard and into the Refuge proper.

"How did it go with Drew?" Corinthia asked, out of true curiosity and to delay talking about her own evening just a little bit longer.

"As you know," Stevie said, " there is absolutely nothing open in Shadow Ridge after a certain hour, unless you count liquor stores and superstores."

"True," Corinthia said.

"And I don't think Drew or I were quite ready for the your-place-or-mine conversation."

"Of course," Corinthia agreed, with more calm than she felt, because she was already beginning to wonder how she would explain Rosemary coming back to her place and renovating her yard, and also how that was most definitely not a euphemism.

"So we looked up movie showtimes and found out they were doing that classic cinema thing at the movie theater—"

"Oh, yeah? Which one?" Movies, like books, were stories, and Corinthia couldn't get enough of stories.

"A comedy from the forties about a guy who hides a mermaid from his wife," Stevie said. "Really funny. We shared a bucket of popcorn, and I think we were kind of snuggling the whole time, with our shoulders."

"Did you brush hands in the popcorn?" Corinthia asked, secretly grateful that her life was at least slightly less complicated than the plot of a screwball comedy.

"You bet we did."

"Who was trying harder to make that happen? You or her?"

"I like to think it was a draw," Stevie said, with a self-satisfied air. "What about you? Did you have a wild night—or, at least, a wild night, for Corinthia?"

"I resemble that remark," Corinthia said. "Nothing too wild. Just..." And she confessed to all of it, because they were about to go in the backyard anyway, and Stevie would see the evidence for herself.

"Another *sleepover*?" Stevie said, when Corinthia was done.

Corinthia blinked. "Did you miss the part about magically growing a new forest in my backyard?"

"Sure, sure. Forest, backyard, got it. But you had her sleep in your papasan chair?"

"I didn't *have* her do anything. She wanted to sleep there. She said it was like a nest."

"I see," Stevie said. "And you, what, slept in your bed? By yourself?"

"I believe that was clear in the first place, yes."

"Man," Stevie said. "That's a slow burn."

"I thought you liked controlled burns."

"Yeah, for forests, not my love life."

"Well, it's my love life," Corinthia said, feeling oddly proud but also slightly embarrassed at the same time.

"Aw!" Stevie threw her arms around Corinthia and squeezed her. "You have a love life!"

Corinthia smiled to herself as she was crushed with the strength of true friendship, then politely pointed out, a little breathlessly, that she couldn't breathe.

"I'm so happy for you!" Stevie cried. Then she let go. "Is Rosemary coming to the Wildlife Festival?"

"Yes, I already asked her. Come on," Corinthia said, leading the way. "Let me show you the back before Drew gets here to work on the fence again."

They made their way around back via the side yard. Like the front yard, it still looked just as it always had. But where the side yard would normally have opened up to the full backyard, there was an arch of trees, like a gateway, and the beginning of a white sand path.

"Whoa," Stevie said.

"I know," Corinthia said, as they walked through the arch. "I can hardly believe it myself, even after seeing it last night. There's something different about seeing it in the daytime. I think," she mused, "that at night it seemed like it would disappear with the sun."

Stevie stopped to marvel at a shrub filled with fragrant flowers. Her fingers grazed the petals. "I have to admit I'm a little bit jealous."

Corinthia did not quite have the words to express her deep sense of gratitude for her own good fortune, so she remained silent and let Stevie stroll the miniature maze slowly, like it was an art museum filled with treasures.

When they reached where the small path opened up into the Refuge itself, Stevie stopped. "Oh, Corinthia," she said. "It's all so beautiful."

"I know," Corinthia said. It was at that moment she noticed her own dress shirt hanging from the top of the fence. She collected it, brought it swiftly and covertly to her face to breathe its scent, and then folded it fussily over her arm as if nothing out of the ordinary had just happened.

When Corinthia's phone dinged to herald Drew's arrival, it startled both of them.

Stevie jogged off to collect Drew from the driveway.

When the two of them returned to the opening into the Refuge, Drew stopped short. "Dude," she said, "what happened to your yard?"

"I re-landscaped it," Corinthia said.

"Huh." Drew dropped her tool bag by the fence, then crouched where the fence met the ground. "You know the only thing holding this up is the trees?"

"Really?" Corinthia said, feigning innocence, and probably not very well.

"What happened to the posts I put up?"

"Cracked, I guess?"

Drew stood up, removed her ball cap, and rubbed her forehead. "I mean, I guess I can work around these trees, put up the posts again..." She stepped back and eyeballed the center of the fence. "Open it up right here, gate swings open"—she pantomimed the motion—"just enough space, I think."

"Perfect," Corinthia said.

Drew began measuring and taking notes. "You wanna tell me what you've actually been up to?"

"What do you mean?"

Drew thumped a skinny tree trunk with her hand. "They don't sell these things at a nursery, and they sure don't grow overnight."

Corinthia hesitated. It wasn't that she didn't trust Drew; it was that explaining personal things was difficult, and she had a tendency to freeze up.

"You know what?" said Drew, with a mischievous expression, "I'll ask Stevie. Give her enough food and she'll tell me anything."

"I will not," Stevie said. "Wait—what kind of food are we talking about, here?"

"Good to know you would sell me out for a hot dog," Corinthia said. "I'll tell you," she added, to Drew, "but you have to promise not to tell anyone else."

"I swear on my mother," Drew said.

"Your mother is alive and well and living in Poughkeepsie," Corinthia pointed out.

"That's even better, isn't it?"

It probably was, so Corinthia filled her in.

"So you're splitting your time between your two places," Drew said, when Corinthia finished.

"Why is everyone more interested in my living arrangements than the unbelievable transformation of my backyard?"

"Did you formally ask this woman out yet?" Drew said. "I mean, you're sleeping at her place, she's sleeping at yours, you eat breakfast together, shouldn't you maybe make it official?"

"That's what I said," Stevie chimed in.

"I haven't figured out how to bring it up yet," Corinthia admitted.

Drew looked like she might laugh, but then she quickly became serious, even earnest. "Look, Corinthia. My friend. All you have to do is say, 'Hey, mama, how's about we make it official?' And then she says yes, and you give her a big smackeroo. You get what I'm saying?"

"It's not that simple."

"Why not?"

"Well, for one thing," Corinthia said. "She's from... *over there*." Corinthia gestured toward the Refuge. "I'm from *over here*."

"So what?"

"She thinks she's a *bird*."

"Again, so what?"

So what, indeed. Corinthia didn't actually care whether or not Rosemary was a bird; she only had the lingering suspicion that she was *supposed* to care, that a normal person *would* care, but Corinthia was beginning to suspect that she herself might be slightly different.

"She reads books like you?" Drew continued.

"Yes..."

"She seems to know what she wants?"

"I think so."

"Then if she's not cool with something she can just turn into a bird and fly away, so what are you worried about?"

Corinthia had never thought about it that way. In one sense it was relieving. In another sense it filled her with cold-sweat panic that Rosemary might want to fly away. "Do you think… do you think she's waiting for me to say something?"

Drew marked the fence in several places, seemingly taking time to think about her response. "Kids today, some of them don't like to put labels on relationships. People our age, though, we're old-school. We gotta know where we stand."

"Are birds old-school?" Stevie asked.

"The oldest," Drew said. "They come from dinosaurs, right?"

"I'm going to see her again at the Wildlife Festival," Corinthia said. She had envisioned arm-in-arm strolls, sugary fried treats, and perhaps a souvenir photo with Jay the Scrub Jay, the event's mascot, who was always played by one of the library or environmental center staff in costume.

"Drew will be there with her food truck," Stevie said. "I'll be doing guided hikes most of the time, but when I get a break I'm coming out for snacks. And I'm going to ride on the eco-buggy. And maybe go to the raptor demonstration if I have time."

"Who's wearing the scrub jay costume this year?" Corinthia asked. Every year, someone had to wear the stifling scrub jay costume. She'd done her time once or twice.

Stevie stared at her.

"What?" Corinthia said.

"Didn't you know?"

"Didn't I know what?"

Stevie looked anywhere but at Corinthia. "We went over the roster from previous years..."

"And?"

"And everyone else has had a turn in the rotation and now it's back to you."

"I am not wearing six feet of fake feathers and a bird head that smells like gym socks."

"I'm afraid that you are."

Corinthia fell silent. Perhaps it was unreasonable to fume at the injustice of the world over having to wear a hot and stinky bird suit, but Corinthia did a very good job of fuming anyway.

"You don't have to wear it the whole time. You can take breaks. Go to the native plant talk. Heck, you can give one yourself, now," she added, gesturing to the backyard.

"I did want to see the raptor demonstration—"

"Don't wear the bird suit!" Drew said. "The raptor might think you're a snack."

"Very funny," Corinthia said.

24

On the day of the Wildlife Festival, Corinthia stood in the largest stall of the library restroom and faced down the uninhabited bird costume like an old enemy. Was there anything more lacking in dignity, she thought, than climbing into such a monstrosity in the inelegant confines of a bathroom stall?

But there was nothing for it. Corinthia knew her duty; it was right and fair that it was her turn, and Corinthia could never say no to *right* and *fair*.

She tugged off her shoes and set them neatly to the side. She stripped down into a tank top and a lightweight pair of stretchy shorts, feeling uncomfortably uncovered. She pulled the costume itself off the hanger—the head hung on the purse hook—and shook it out, hoping to dislodge any spiders that might have taken up residence over the last year of disuse.

Then she carefully gathered it up, stepped into one leg, and then stepped into the other.

She had put the bird costume successfully over her ankles. Unfortunately, this did not improve the overall lack of dignity. So she drew it up over her bare legs and over her torso before stuffing her arms down the bulky sleeves. There were hand covers, too, like oversized blue mittens, but these also hung on the purse hook, beneath the bird head.

Corinthia reached for the back zipper—flailed for the back zipper—and finally realized that someone else was going to have to zip her up. She sighed. "Stevie!" she called.

While she waited, she stepped into her sneakers and looked in the mirror.

She looked neither like herself nor like a bird, but something in the middle of transforming.

The bathroom door squeaked open.

Corinthia turned from the mirror and unlatched the stall door. "The zipper," she said, as Stevie bounded in.

"Turn around," Stevie said.

Corinthia obeyed, and heard the long, metallic zipper slide closed. There was a snap as Stevie closed the final button that disguised the zipper with a cover of blue fur.

"All set," Stevie said.

"Do I put the head on first, or the mittens?"

"Maybe the head first, so it's easy to adjust."

Corinthia stared the bird head in the eyes, then lifted it off the hook. She held it over her head, realizing she was also holding her breath, and had to start breathing purposely before lowering the bird head over her own. Immediately she lost most of her field of vision, and what she had left was filtered through an almost opaque mesh. "Is it straight?" she asked.

Stevie stepped back and peered at Corinthia. "I think so."

"I feel like the taxidermied hawk."

"You look amazing," Stevie said. "Now the mittens."

Corinthia held out her hands and allowed Stevie to maneuver the mittens onto them. "Stop enjoying this."

"I really can't."

"At least try to *pretend* you're not enjoying this."

"I'm not that good of an actress."

Corinthia turned toward the mirror again, to see—as best she could—the final effect. "This is not what I imagined it would be like to be a bird," she said.

"How often have you imagined it?"

"I've had dreams about it for days." Corinthia turned her head a little to the left and right, trying to see through the wide-set bird eyes. "There was a lot more flying involved." Just remembering the feeling of flight made her forget, for one airy moment, the weight of the costume.

"Come on," Stevie said, gathering up Corinthia's things. "Time for all scrub jays to take flight. Boy, your purse is heavier than normal," she added.

"I brought a book," Corinthia said, gruffly, not sharing that it was actually a gift-wrapped present for Rosemary. She allowed Stevie to take her arm and guide out of the stall, out of the bathroom, and finally outside, into the exuberance of the Wildlife Festival.

The eco-buggy was parked out front. The buggy itself was a large trailer, open to the air, with built-in wooden benches along the sides and a metal roof to provide shade from the sun. It was hitched to a truck, ready to carry passengers through the Refuge on the widest of the white sand trails.

Upbeat pop music filled the air. Aromas of food made it through the breathing holes in the costume head and mixed with the smell of the suit, which made Corinthia feel a bit ill. Thank goodness the fall day had dawned cool and stayed cool, or Corinthia would have been roasted like a chicken.

There were pop-up tents in every direction in the parking lot, but she could not make out the details very well. She simply let Stevie guide her to the tent with the photo backdrop depicting the Refuge.

When at last she had reached the proper tent, she found George, the certified forest bathing guide, waiting. He would be her helper, as Stevie had to gallivant off to the Refuge to lead the hikes. There was a folding chair for each of them. Corinthia decided—virtuously, she thought—that she would remain standing for as long as she could, since the costume was shown to its best effect when standing, and wouldn't it look odd for a scrub jay to sit in a folding chair? She owed something to the people who attended, and if it resulted in sore feet or sore everything, she was willing to sacrifice. No one would ever say Corinthia did not do her duty.

She was spotted almost immediately by every family with young children in the vicinity. They all converged into an impromptu line, which George managed with good humor.

For a while, Corinthia smiled for every photo, until she realized no one could see her smile, and at last she allowed her tired facial muscles to relax.

She did not know when to expect Rosemary, and she couldn't see, so every new person approaching was a mystery that resolved into disappointment when they were not Rosemary.

Every so often George coaxed her to go inside, to take off the costume head and mittens, to rest and drink chilled, brightly-colored sports drinks. Then it was time to suit up again.

Because she could not see a clock or her own phone to tell the time, she asked George to let her know when it was almost time for the scheduled raptor demonstration. She would need time to undress and time to walk over to the high school athletic field across the street, which was the only space large enough to hold the demonstration.

But even the raptor demonstration was forgotten when she heard a sweet, familiar voice calling her name.

Even with her vision obscured, she could see Rosemary was wearing the fluttery dress she'd worn on the first day they'd met. Corinthia waved her "wing" enthusiastically as Rosemary approached.

"My very own Corinthia-bird!" Rosemary exclaimed.

Corinthia smiled until her face hurt even though no one could see.

George offered to use his own phone to take the picture, since Rosemary had none and Corinthia had left hers safely inside the library.

They moved into position, side by side in front of the Refuge backdrop. Rosemary's arm went around Corinthia's blue-feathered waist, and Corinthia's wing went over Rosemary's blue silk-clad shoulders. This, Corinthia thought, was even better than a prom photo.

"Say 'scrub jays'!" George prompted.

"Scrub jays!" they said.

When the moment was captured, George gave them a thumbs-up.

"Can I meet you after the raptor demonstration?" Corinthia asked Rosemary.

"Of course!" Rosemary said. "Where shall we meet?"

"How about Drew's D-Lites?"

"Sounds delicious," Rosemary agreed. Corinthia couldn't see, but she heard the distinct sound of an air kiss somewhere near the outside of her bird face. "Bye, Corinthia-bird!"

Corinthia felt slightly dizzied, and couldn't attribute it to the costume alone.

Many more people came for photos. Corinthia posed, and waved her wings at passers-by, until it was time to retire for a real break. She swapped her tank and shorts for her regular clothes, and left the sweaty things hanging up to air while she went off to the raptor demonstration.

When Corinthia emerged from the Shadow Ridge Library and crossed the parking lot, through the Wildlife Festival, she did not see Rosemary or Stevie. Drew, she assumed, was dishing out hot dogs and cold drinks at her truck. So it would be a solo trip, which suited Corinthia fine. Rosemary could not go that far from the Refuge; not yet, anyway. Maybe next year.

A road separated the library and environmental center complex from Shadow Ridge High School. Corinthia paused carefully by the side of the road, looked both ways, then hurried across.

Through the gate was a vast green field. A permanent pavilion off to the side of the field held a small crowd. Corinthia made her way through the visitors to the perches for the visiting raptors.

There was a red-shouldered hawk, an owl, and a bald eagle on display. Rope barriers had been put up to keep curious children (and foolish adults) from getting too close. The birds, Corinthia noticed, had wickedly sharp beaks.

She had been very excited, but the more she looked at the birds, the more her excitement gained an edge, sharp like a paper cutter in the library office.

She had heard an owl in the Refuge before, at night. In her own neighborhood, she had seen and heard several hawks. Once she had even spotted a bald eagle flying overhead toward its nest in a nearby phone tower.

The knowledge that these birds of prey made themselves at home nearby gave Corinthia a strange sensation in her gut. She did not recognize the feeling for what it was, yet. Only that she didn't particularly like it.

Nevertheless she tried to enjoy the brief talk given by the bird experts who helped rehabilitate birds and educate the public. In addition to sharp beaks, the birds had keen eyesight, excellent hearing, and sharp talons that were strong enough to crush bones. Corinthia found herself with a dry mouth and yet an uncontrollable urge to swallow. She wished she had brought a bottle of the neon sports drink.

These raptors were everywhere, the speaker was saying, and they maintained the balance of nature by hunting bugs, snakes, rabbits, fish, and even other birds.

Other birds.

Everything froze, or so it seemed to Corinthia. The speaker may have continued speaking, the birds might have been shifting from side to side on their perches, their yellow eyes bright and staring; the people may have continued to murmur and mill about, but to Corinthia it was all a tableau accompanied by the sound of her heartbeat in her own ears.

Rosemary.

She had spent days humoring the story that Rosemary was a bird, never once letting herself believe—not really—that the *story* could also be *true*.

She had even congratulated herself on being so accepting and open-minded when, in fact, what she had actually done was glide right over the possibility; to never truly imagine that it might actually be real.

But *what if*?

What if it wasn't a charming quirk? What if there was no such thing as an adorable delusion?

What if it was real?

What if Rosemary was one of the birds in the Refuge, forever vulnerable to sharp beaks and sharp talons that were strong enough to crush bones?

The remaining sports drink in her belly roiled and threatened to reappear.

Her heartbeat filled her ears as the world unfroze and the crowd moved toward the open field. They were eager for the flight demonstration. Corinthia, on the other hand, no longer wanted to see a perfect avian killing machine on the wing. She backed up and stumbled off the raised edge of the pavilion floor.

She had to get away. To get somewhere else.

To get...

To Rosemary.

Yes, that was what she must do. Corinthia would talk to her. She would convince Rosemary to never become a bird again. To stay human. To stay safe forever. There were hawks and owls out there, she would say. You have to be safe.

I will keep you safe.

But what if Rosemary would not agree?

Corinthia made it to the sidewalk along the road that separated the high school from the library and environmental center complex.

She stopped, unable to process the cars flying past, unable to gauge when to cross. None of it made sense. So she simply stood, body unmoving, thoughts racing.

In all the stories, she knew, if you stole a swan maiden's clothing, she could no longer transform. Rosemary herself had said it: *I must always keep this with me,* she had said, *or else I cannot change form.*

So many pretty outfits. So many happy memories. The fluttery dress on the day they met. The pantsuit with the jeweled buckle on Halloween. Pajamas when she fell in the pond, a sarong on the night in the green cottage, a prom dress at the concert where they danced. Each a work of art like Rosemary herself, inextricable from her one-of-a-kind nature.

And all Corinthia had to do—

Take the silks. Take the gems.

Hide them.

And Rosemary would be human forever.

Corinthia could contrive something, she knew. And then: safety. No more fear of hawks.

No more flying.

And as she imagined her hands full of stolen silk, her palms pierced by the elegant gems in their metal settings, Corinthia closed her eyes in shame.

In her bag, back at the library, lay a gift-wrapped book, specially purchased. A gift to make it official, as Drew had said. A literary offer of love, carefully wrapped in shiny, colorful paper.

Alien Space Lesbians.

A story of two women from different worlds.

Corinthia had finally finished it.

She had been surprised by the ending. The space alien hadn't moved to Earth; the human hadn't moved to space. The human had not grounded her space captain beloved, had not forbidden her to ever venture again among the stars. The space captain had not dragged her human away from the only home she'd ever known. Instead, life went on as they traveled between their different worlds, loving each other dearly, orbiting each other rather than one particular star or another.

Because love isn't fear, Corinthia realized.

Love is flying free.

She opened her eyes and found tears on her cheeks.

Across the street lay everything she loved. The Shadow Ridge Library. The Shadow Ridge Environmental Center. The Pollinator Garden and the Outdoor Amphitheater.

And beyond, the Refuge. The place she'd feared. The place she'd changed. The place she had learned, at last, to let go.

All of it was home, from the white sand to the sky and everything in between, and she would steward it, fight for it, and yes, *love* all of it until the day she died.

The dark thoughts, and the shame of them, burned away like mist in the morning.

No more fear. Just love.

Love for Beaufort. Love for Stevie and Drew. Love for chocolate and books, creatures and trees.

Love for Rosemary.

Whether Rosemary would accept her love or not, Corinthia could do nothing but flap her own wings and hope to fly, to give a gift and expect nothing in return, to finally express how she really felt, unafraid of what might happen after.

She was light on her feet. She could feel the lifting sensation in her mind as if it were only one strong, fresh breeze away from being real. Had she flapped her arms just then, she could have almost flown.

The traffic cleared, and Corinthia crossed the road.

25

Corinthia had never felt so frustrated in a crowd. People everywhere, and Rosemary nowhere in sight. Corinthia went on tiptoe, which didn't help, then hurried from tent to tent asking everyone she knew if they had seen a woman in a billowing blue silk dress.

They had not.

She had the wrapped book in her hands. She had only to wait, she knew, for Rosemary to arrive at Drew's food truck, but what she had to say needed to be said properly, in the right environment. But how would she track Rosemary down?

She stopped. She stood in the middle of the Wildlife Festival and felt the sand deep below the asphalt, felt the trees beyond the library complex. Of course she could find Rosemary, just like she had found Mr. Thriller on the day of the local author festival.

Hello, she thought, her mind full of forest. *Remember me?*

The Refuge reared up in her mind like a happy dog greeting a friend.

Awareness unfolded: first of the sand beneath everything, then the trees and bushes connected to it, then the busy birds and snakes and everything else that made homes there, and finally a rush of humanity all around and in the Refuge itself. Corinthia herself was simultaneously just a person standing in the midst of it all, and she was also the breeze that traveled through it, swaying and spinning like a dancer at the concert.

There was George, who had slipped into the bird suit and was having the time of his life.

There was Stevie, atop the highest hill in the Refuge, admiring the view.

There was Drew, in her food truck, slinging D-Lites.

There was Beaufort, curled up at home, dreaming doggy dreams.

And was that... Mr. Thriller? Inside the Shadow Ridge Library, browsing the romance paperbacks?

Corinthia chuckled to herself and kept searching.

So many people. So many animals. So many plants. But there, at last, was the one she searched for: in the Refuge, in a section Corinthia had never hiked, but not too far from familiar trails.

Corinthia set off, following the north star of her own heart. It would guide her to the center of any Castle Adventure.

The maze wrapped her in its embrace. She was in the arms of the oaks, the loving hands of the lyonia bushes. Overhead the sky shone scrub jay blue. Corinthia did not know how she had ever been afraid of this place, did not know why she'd stayed away from it for so long; she only knew that now she rushed into its embrace like she was being welcomed home for the first time, understood and accepted at last.

The green walls rose around her. Green mansions formed and faded like daydreams: there was Drew's food truck, there were the library shelves. There was the shape of her own little green house, *Lucky Charms* chic, and Corinthia felt very lucky indeed.

Past the Ephemeral Wetland. Past the Woodland Theater. Off to a tiny trail that opened up suddenly, as if it were a secret passageway, and led to a white sand clearing shaped like a perfect circle. When she entered the clearing it seemed as if the passageway closed behind her. The path was hidden.

She was alone.

But where was Rosemary?

Her senses had told her Rosemary was here, and with full certainty Corinthia knew that she had not been wrong.

And then a scrub jay fluttered to the center of the white sand circle.

If birds could learn to recognize people, so too could people learn to recognize birds. This one Corinthia knew. This one Corinthia had met over and over again, in the day and the night, and she would never mistake it for any other.

With the book in hand, Corinthia slowly moved closer. "It's okay," she said. "I won't hurt you. I would never hurt you."

The bird looked up at her, bright black eyes sharp. It cocked its head.

Corinthia lowered herself to her knees. She placed the wrapped book on the sand. "I brought you something."

The bird hopped forward and tapped the shiny wrapping paper with its beak, seemingly investigating.

Corinthia had come so far. Had ventured so much. And yet, as she kneeled on the sand in front of a scrub jay, she could not find the words.

So she closed her eyes. She held her hands over the sand, a supplicant as much to her own feelings as the Refuge itself. The trees surrounded the clearing like cathedral columns; she breathed the wind; she listened to the bird cries in the distance, and the far-off hub-bub of the Wildlife Festival. *Relax,* she thought, and imagined Rosemary's arms around her.

Then it came to her—the warmth, the glow, the life itself waiting to break free—and roots unfurled into the sand around her. Stems grew and reached for the sky. Pink and purple flowers burst into generous bunches of tiny blooms, smelling like honey and perfume.

More, she thought.

And the Refuge, eager to please, rocketed more of the flowering plants upward until Corinthia, without looking, could feel them filling the whole clearing. When a few bees descended to the newly-grown blossoms, their hum did not strike fear in Corinthia. They only reminded her of hymns sung softly.

When she opened her eyes, the scrub jay was gone.

The new-grown flowers bobbed in the breeze.

And Rosemary stood before Corinthia, an angel draped in silver-blue silk.

She reached down and picked up the gift. She smiled. "Is this what I think it is?"

"Rosemary," Corinthia said. She stayed on her knees and took Rosemary's hand. The words still would not come, only Rosemary's name, so she repeated it and pressed kisses on Rosemary's hand. It was always possible that she would look up and Rosemary would be gone, a beautiful bird flown into the wilderness once more—but there was no more fear in

Corinthia's heart; only gratitude for every moment they had already shared, and this made Corinthia strong enough to bear anything.

Instead of flying away, Rosemary sank to the sand to join Corinthia, and both of them were surrounded by flowers topped with the occasional fat bumblebee.

Faced with Rosemary so close, Corinthia's extensive vocabulary deserted her entirely, so when Rosemary hushed her and stroked her cheek, Corinthia gratefully let go of attempting to say something clever.

Rosemary's eyes were like the night sky, full of stars. Full of mischief, too, as she leaned closer and murmured in Corinthia's ear. "Hey, mama," she said, "how's about we make it official?"

Corinthia couldn't help laughing. "Were you listening to us?"

"I didn't mean to, but scrub jays have excellent hearing. What do you say?"

Only one word was needed. Never mind that her whole body shouted it, that the Refuge echoed it, that Shadow Ridge itself rumbled in harmony with it. She had to say it.

And she did.

"Yes," Corinthia said.

The simple affirmative made boldness bloom in her like the pink and purple flowers. She closed the remaining distance between them, and this time when she kissed Rosemary, her bird-woman did not disappear and leave a Jay Watch t-shirt behind. Rosemary kissed her right back, and the buzzing of the bees was no longer just any hymn but an ode to joy. *Stevie was right,* Corinthia thought. *Everything is magic.*

And then even her own busy internal monologue, constantly observing, ever analyzing, fell blissfully quiet as the kiss deepened. Every leaf in the Refuge shivered with their shared delight; the water rippled joyfully in the Ephemeral Wetlands; and even the little gray snake poked its head out of its burrow to see what all the fuss was about.

When Corinthia finally drew back it was with great reluctance, so she left kisses on Rosemary's cheek and a few down her neck, to tide them both over until later. "I should go relieve George," Corinthia said.

"Let the forest bathing man stay in costume," Rosemary said. "He's enjoying himself."

This was true. Corinthia could not argue it. But as romantic as the flowered clearing was, she could not help but think that either of their green cottages might be much more comfortable. "We should celebrate," she said, standing up and helping Rosemary to her feet. "Let me get you something to eat."

"You mean the loaded hot dogs and the frothy, creamy orange drinks you were telling me about?"

"The very same."

"Mmm! Almost as delicious as—" She stole a kiss, and it turned into mutual theft which lasted a minute or two.

"The nice thing," Corinthia said, cherishing how she could say this softly into her beloved's ear, "is that we get to have both."

The walk back to the Shadow Ridge Library had the air of a triumphant recessional, the birds playing them out with jazzy panache. Corinthia and Rosemary emerged into the bustle of the Wildlife Festival and were faced with almost too many activities to choose from, although any activity could have made it the most perfect day ever, because they had each other.

So they giggled their way through the scrub jay presentation; rode the eco-buggy with the wind in their smiling faces; and admired the native plants display, arguing cheerfully over which was the prettiest. They both got into a photo with scrub jay George. They found Stevie, who gave Corinthia a covert thumbs-up, and all of them went together to Drew's food truck.

Frothy, creamy orange drinks had never tasted sweeter. Loaded hot dogs had never tasted more savory. There were more educational presentations to be seen, and a few more rides on the eco-buggy to be had, before the festival finally drew to a close.

Slowly the crowd dwindled, and the sun sank toward the horizon, and night threw its coverlet over the sky, until at last everyone but Corinthia and Rosemary had packed up and stolen away into the small town of Shadow Ridge, where (almost) nothing ever happened.

Then they walked into the Refuge together, where there were stars all around.

And they were extremely happy.

26

BEAUFORT'S EPILOGUE

There were regular days, which in Beaufort's experience included a great deal of lounging, scratching, sniffing, and the occasional stroll down the street; and then there were days that didn't match up with anything in his dog years of experience. Today was such a day.

The backyard, which had been acceptably grassy not too long ago, and soft on his sensitive foot pads, had been transformed into a scent-filled paradise of new plants. The grass had been replaced with twisty pathways of white sand, which were great fun to explore, even if the sand tickled, and occasionally got tracked into his little bed, which his beloved Corinthia would then have to shake out.

And now the backyard had even more new things. Someone had placed great heaps of food on a table, including a towering cake that smelled so much of sugar, fresh butter, and vanilla that Beaufort could not help but lick his chops every time he caught a whiff of it on the air.

But every time he tried to climb up for a better sniff, and maybe a taste or two or four, someone shooed him down. So he wove his way through feet and ankles, old instincts of the hunt converted to modern use looking for dropped morsels.

The guests were showing their teeth quite a lot. Beaufort had learned that this meant happiness, and as such he had no fear, only canine curiosity, as he made his way through the small crowd. One of the guests laughed, spilling a splash of her drink, and the sparkling gold liquid fell in a rainshower of shining drops on Beaufort's nose. It was not precisely to Beaufort's taste, being a bit on the sour side, but he licked his own nose anyway, to be thorough.

There were guests who smelled like they spent much of their time around books, and guests who smelled like they socialized with turtles and snakes. Beaufort did not discriminate. He had learned that a soulful look could earn snacks, and if that didn't work, perhaps going on two legs and begging would.

His mistresses were dressed very differently that day.

Rosemary's blue dress trailed the ground, and would probably have to have the sand shaken out later just like his bed. She had flowers in her hair, and flowers in her hands, which struck Beaufort as odd, because flowers were usually found on or near the ground.

Corinthia's bright white jacket shone like the moon, which made Beaufort have to stop himself from an instinctual howl. She had a small bunch of flowers attached to the jacket.

They, too, were showing their teeth quite a lot, and this pleased Beaufort, because when his humans felt joy, all was right with the world. And sometimes he got extra treats.

They were standing by the closed back gate, beyond which he was not allowed to venture. Drew stood before them. Beaufort highly approved of Drew, who sometimes smelled of delicious hot dogs, and sometimes snuck him tidbits. Stevie stood nearby holding another bunch of flowers. Why humans insisted on wearing or carrying something they couldn't eat mystified Beaufort, but he was willing to accept their little eccentricities.

He was also mildly distracted by all the chattering blue birds perched on the back fence.

And now Corinthia and Rosemary were holding hands, speaking in turn to repeat something that Drew was saying. It was not such supreme barking as Beaufort could do, but it sounded nice to his sensitive ears.

When they were finished speaking, Corinthia and Rosemary kissed.

This, Beaufort understood well. There were things you could only learn about someone by kissing their face. And in fact he needed to be involved, so he galloped, paws a-flying, ears a-flapping, to where they stood.

They both crouched to greet him, and he could hardly decide who to kiss first, so he hopped up and down on his back legs trying to kiss them both at the same time. This made them laugh.

He found himself swept up in Corinthia's arms, close to her face, which made things even easier, and when Rosemary leaned in and scratched behind his ears, he kissed her too.

Today is the best day ever, he thought.

And so would be tomorrow, and every day after that.

Corinthia's Hot Cocoa Recipe

I f you'd like to be fancy, you can use Guittard Cocoa Rouge cocoa powder and Penzeys Mexican Vanilla Extract, but any good-quality cocoa powder and pure vanilla extract will work great. You can whisk in a pinch of spice, like cinnamon or cardamom, for variety, or top with whipped cream for extra decadence. You can also make it dairy-free by using your favorite plant milk. Makes two small servings or one large serving!

1/3 cup water
1/3 cup unsweetened cocoa powder
1/3 cup sugar
1 pinch salt
1/4 teaspoon pure vanilla extract
1 1/2 cups milk, or more

1. In a small saucepan, combine the water, cocoa powder, sugar, and a pinch of salt. Whisk to combine. Add the vanilla extract.

2. Heat the saucepan over medium heat. Whisk briskly for a minute or two until the mixture is smooth, glossy, and warm.

3. Pour in 1 1/2 cups of milk and whisk until frothy and slightly steamy. Do not boil. Taste, and add more milk if the hot chocolate is too strong for you. Pour into mugs and enjoy!

Acknowledgements

First, I would like to thank the staff and volunteers of the Lyonia Environmental Center for patiently putting up with all of my questions about the Florida scrub. Without this wonderful museum and its natural wonderland, the Lyonia Preserve, I would not have been able to write this book. If there are any factual errors in this book, they are entirely my fault, either due to my own mistakes or because I sprinkled pixie dust on the facts to make them suit the story.

In addition, the staff of the Deltona Regional Library and the entire Volusia County Public Library system kept me well-supplied with books throughout the writing process. I am so grateful for public libraries.

Much love goes to my local bookstores: Spellbound Bookstore, White Rose Books & More, The New Romantics, Spiral Circle Bookstore & More, The Black Rabbit Book Bar, Sunshine Book Company, Novel Tea Book Shop, Fern & Fable

Books, The Family Book Shop, and Barnes & Noble Plaza Venezia. Thank you for being awesome.

To my fellow authors, both in person and online, thank you for all of your support. We're all in this together.

To my early readers, a thousand thanks. Sometimes it feels like I'm sculpting clay while wearing a blindfold, and you helped me to see what I was actually making. I couldn't have done it without you.

To the readers who follow me from one magical story to another, thank you for taking this journey with me.

And to my family: For years, you've watched me transform into a cave troll who hunches over a keyboard while drinking too much coffee and devouring snacks. I love you all. Thanks for being you.

Book Club Guide

1. How does the setting of *A Nest of Magic* affect the story? Is there a natural setting you would like to see depicted in a fantasy story?

2. Did you notice any clues that hinted at Rosemary's true nature before it was revealed? If you were able to transform, what would you transform into and why?

3. Corinthia loves books and chocolate. If you were a main character, what would be your two most noticeable obsessions?

4. Over the course of the story, several magical powers are revealed. What would your magical powers be, if you could choose any?

5. The story explores themes of love and nature. Can

you think of any other books, movies, or TV shows that share these themes? Who would you cast to star in an adaptation of this book?

6. What do you think happens after the end of the story?

AUTHOR'S NOTE

For more information on the rare and beautiful Florida scrub jay, I recommend *Florida Scrub-Jay: Field Notes on a Vanishing Bird* by Mark Jerome Walters. For more about the Florida scrub, *Florida's Uplands* by Ellie Whitney and D. Bruce Means has excellent information and colorful photos to enjoy. And if you'd like to try forest bathing for yourself, pick up *Your Guide to Forest Bathing* by M. Amos Clifford.

As Rosemary says, the more time you spend in the forest, the more you will understand. So get out there and explore!

ALSO BY KATE MOSEMAN

Silver Spells
Silver Charms
Silver Dreams
Silver Shadows

Spells and Sandwiches
Masks and Mirrors
Flames and Frying Pans
Witch and Wolfhound

A Good Demon Is Hard to Find
A Witch's Work Is Never Done
An Angel in My Teacup

Roller Coaster Romance